PACK TO THE WALL

HER BAD BOY WOLVES: BOOK 1

TESSA COLE

CLARA WILS

Gryphon's Gate Publishing

Pack to the Wall

Copyright © 2024 Tessa Cole & Clara Wils

Gryphon's Gate Publishing
550 King St. N.
PO Box 42088 Conestoga
Waterloo, ON
N2L 6K5

Print ISBN: 978-1-990587-44-3

JANE

"Mom! Milo's lost it!" Izzy's panicked voice echoed through the house as she burst through the front door. "He's gone to talk to those bikers!"

My two kids *should* have been waiting for the school bus. I'd been about to head to work, purse in hand, when I'd heard the terrible roar of motorcycles rumbling up the street.

Dread twisted my gut.

"What—?" I gasped and rushed over to peek out the front door.

Milo flagged down the twenty or so bikers and boldly moved toward them as they stopped in front of my house.

Panic surged through me. My heart leaped into my throat as fear washed over me. Images flashed through my mind of the rough and unpredictable vagrants — who'd taken up residence in the forest at the far end of the street for the last couple months — roughing up my boy.

"What's he thinking?" I breathed, my mind racing

with worry. I couldn't fathom why my thirteen-year-old baby would want to talk to those ruffians. It didn't matter. I needed to keep my family safe.

With a mix of anxiety and determination, I reached into my purse and clenched the cold grip of the small gun I'd reluctantly bought. Violence and guns were never my preference, but the menacing presence of the bikers had backed me into a corner. My family's safety was paramount, and I was willing to do whatever it took to protect them.

"Izzy, get inside! Hide in your room. Now!"

There was something hard in my voice, something that surprised even me. But my sixteen-year-old daughter listened to me for once and obeyed, disappearing down the hall.

I pulled the small gun out of my purse with a trembling hand. As much as I loathed these things, I'd made sure I knew how to use it before I'd left the store. I slid back the top piece to load a bullet from the clip into the chamber, then flipped off the safety. Shuddering out a long breath, I put it back in my purse and made my way outside on trembling legs.

"Milo!" I called across the front lawn, trying to keep my voice steady despite the fear swirling within me. "Get back here now!"

My little boy — okay, he wasn't as little as he used to be since he'd grown almost half a foot over the last year — turned back to me. "Mom? No, it's okay, I—"

"Milo Arthur Myers. Get inside now!" I shouted, my voice sharp. My heart pounded, threatening to leap out of my chest.

The bikers laughed derisively. One of them shouted. "Yeah pup, run to your mommy!"

Milo didn't move, and I couldn't understand what he was doing, why he was so obsessed with this rowdy gang?

I reached him and quickly wrapped one arm around his wiry frame. He was tall, up to my chin now, but he was still my little boy. My grip on the gun tightened in my purse.

"Get inside!" I hissed, spinning us around and pushing him toward the house. Then I turned back to stand between him and those brutes, practically face to face with the bikers.

They were a rough lot with tattoos, muscles, and hard looks. There were several women among them, but the leaders were clearly four older men who had grey hair and stony glares. No, one wasn't glaring. He was leering, eyeing me like a piece of meat and licking his lips.

With my free hand, I clasped my suit jacket closed over my blouse, though there wasn't anything I could do to hide my calves, which were clearly visible below the knee-length skirt.

"Go!" I shouted at them, trying to muster all the courage I had left, hoping that would be enough to get them to leave. Inside, my heart raced, and adrenaline rushed through my veins.

I had no clue why they'd chosen our little dead-end street to take up residence. They'd roar in every evening — usually far too late — and park their bikes on the greenspace just off the closed loop of the street. Then they'd grab some gear and go camp in the forest. The next morning they'd ride out to cruise around Riverside or Shannondale, sometimes even Charles Town.

"Your boy's a little too curious," rumbled the lead biker, an older man with a scruffy beard and cold eyes.

Dear Lord! What had Milo done?

The biggest of the bikers, the one undressing me with his eyes, pulled his gaze from my legs up to where my hand disappeared into my purse. "What you got in there? Pepper spray?" he asked with a laugh.

Not quite, I thought.

"Just go!" I said, my voice trembling. "Please, stay away from my family." *Stay away from our neighborhood! Just leave and never come back!*

But the leader kicked the stand of his bike down and turned off the rumbling engine. His three large cronies did the same. "We take what we want, when we want," the leader said with growling intensity.

My pulse lurched and I took a step back, making the big one laugh.

"And right now, I want to see that boy of yours." The leader heaved himself off his bike and stood.

He was big, an imposing man well over six feet tall and built like one of the wrestlers Milo liked to watch on TV. The other three also got off their bikes. They were all huge, and the one eye-fucking me was monstrous, even taller than the leader and built like a bear.

I stumbled back another step, my grip on the gun tightening.

"No," I said, surprising myself. My voice was far firmer than it had any right to be.

"Mom..." Milo said from behind me.

"No!" I shouted. "Get inside now!" My tone held that hard edge. It had gotten Izzy moving and I hoped it would do the same with Milo.

My ears caught Milo's footfalls behind me, running back toward the house. I hoped he was safely inside, but I wouldn't take my eyes off the four dangerous men in front of me.

"You need to leave," I said, steel in my voice. I had no idea where it was coming from because the rest of me was about to fall apart.

"I don't think so," the leader rumbled, taking a step forward.

"Don't take another step!" I shouted.

The leader gave a grin, parting that scraggly beard. "And if I do?" It was clear he thought I was no threat to him.

"I'll do whatever I have to, to protect my family."

"The broad's got some mettle in her," one of the others said.

"I can beat it out of her," the monstrous one replied, licking his teeth with a grin. "Then I'll fuck her raw. She's a bit old for my tastes, but what the hell."

The leader put an arm out to stop the big guy. "No, Tank."

Tank? Yeah, that name suited the massive bruiser.

The leader sized me up. "You really ready to fight over this?" He clearly didn't think I'd say yes.

Was I ready?

Hell no! But, to protect my family... I'd do anything.

I didn't understand why they wanted Milo so much, but it didn't matter. My jaw tightened, twitching, and for a moment I couldn't speak, sweating through my silken blouse.

"If that's what it takes," I said firmly.

The little gun I'd purchased had twelve shots in it. I hoped that would be enough, because it was becoming clear that I wouldn't be walking away from this. I swallowed, tipping my head up in defiance at the leader.

"You want my son? You'll have to go through me. I'll take you all on if I have to!" I blurted.

The leader's head cocked. "You challenging me, little bird?"

Was I? Those words had sure sounded like a challenge.

"I am." My pulse roared with a nauseating mix of determination and fear.

Something swept through the entire gang of bikers. They gasped and whispered. The three guys with the leader all laughed, even as they stepped back to go sit on their bikes and watch.

"Too bad," Tank said with a sniff. "She's got some nice tits." Then his grin grew. "Maybe I'll fuck her once the boss is done with her, while the body's still warm."

Still warm?

Not happening. No way in hell.

"I accept your challenge, little bird," he laughed as he cracked his neck. "You have no idea what you've just done. We take challenges very seriously in our pack. It's a fight to the death, and whoever wins claims everything the other has. So... yeah, your son's gonna be mine soon enough, and now... so is that sweet little daughter of yours."

He flexed his heavily muscled arms, clearly visible with his sleeveless shirt and vest, and stepped toward me with his hands balled into fists.

To the death?

Claim my children?

If one of us was going to die, it sure as hell wasn't going to be me! I'd never let these beasts touch my kids.

With a scream of determination, I pulled out the gun and squeezed the trigger.

JANE

A LOUD CRACK STARTLED ME, AND THE GUN JUMPED IN MY hand, turning my scream into a yelp of surprise.

The leader grunted, going to one knee as blood blossomed over his jeans.

"What the fu—" was all he got out before I squeezed the trigger a second time, terrified.

My left hand had come up to steady my right. I hadn't really been aiming at anything, and the second shot probably would have taken him in the stomach... if he hadn't been kneeling. Instead, it tore through his neck, and blood sprayed everywhere.

The leader's eyes went wide, and he made a sucking, gasping sound even as I pulled the trigger again.

I hadn't meant to, but with the adrenaline flowing through me my finger had twitched.

The third shot hit him right between the eyes and he fell forward... lifeless.

Oh God oh God oh God oh God!

What had I done...?

I'd killed him.

But I'd had no choice, right?

He'd been about to kill me and take my family and... I'd had to do it, hadn't I?

Fuck, fuck, fuck, fuck!

"Don't any of you come near me!" I screamed, waving the gun around. "Or I'll do the same to you!"

But none of the bikers moved, stunned and frozen in place with shocked, wide eyes.

I glanced down at the leader lying on my lawn. He was still, eyes vacant. There was little doubt in my mind he was dead. Far too much blood flowed onto my grass.

I shook like a tree in a storm, sweating like a fiend, palms slick, but I kept a hold of the gun. It was the only thing protecting me.

"Go!" I screamed at the bikers. "I won, so go!"

"That's not how this works."

I spun to face the new voice, gun wavering before me. The man who got off his bike was younger than the three who'd backed up the leader. Long dark hair hung around a tanned face with a chiseled jaw. Dark blue eyes peered at me. They seemed almost... sad? Built like a champion bodybuilder, covered in tattoos, he raised his well-muscled arms in surrender.

"Didn't you hear what Harley said?" this younger one continued.

He didn't get any closer, which was good, because I was so ready to shoot again. I'd already killed one man today.

"Whoever wins gets everything that belonged to the

other," he said. "You won. This gang belonged to Harley, which means we now belong to you."

The gang was mine?

The gang was *mine*!

"No. I don't want you. Go away!"

The younger one gave a sad smile and shook his head. "We can't. You're our alpha now. We follow you until you're challenged in the same way you challenged Harley. That's the only way you get out of this. But that also means you'd be dead. For better or worse, we're yours now, darlin'."

His words sunk in slowly. The only way to get rid of them was to have someone challenge me, and challenges were to the death, and...

Oh, God!

I waved the gun around at the group of them, wondering why no one was challenging me. Probably because I was still waving a gun around.

"No," I breathed. "I... there has to be..."

"There isn't another way, babe," the young one said with what seemed like a sympathetic shrug. "We're yours now. And you can put down the gun, it's pack law that no one can challenge a new alpha for at least seven days. That gives the alpha a bit of time to show who they really are, prove they're worthy."

Alpha?

One week?

Prove they're worthy?

My mind glitched, unable to take this all in. It was too much.

"Mom?" That one — terror-filled — word from my

daughter nearly broke me. I dropped the gun and collapsed to my knees. Weak and unable to control my movements, I couldn't even bring my trembling arms to my face to cover my tears.

For a moment I thought these ruffians would charge in and tackle me, but they didn't. They just sat there looking at me.

Because I was their leader now?

And they couldn't do anything about it for a week?

"Mom? Are you...? What happened?" Izzy was close behind me, kneeling, her own trembling hands on my shoulders. "Mom?"

"Your mother's a very brave woman who did what she had to, to protect you and your brother." I looked up at the young biker as he drew near. He reached down to me, his calloused palm open. "Need a hand, alpha?"

Tears blurred my vision. All I saw were dark blue eyes: clear and captivating. A sympathetic suffering dwelled in those dark depths. Why was he in pain? And why was he helping me?

I didn't know how or why, but I felt I could trust this one, at least for now. I reached up and the moment my palm landed in his, my shaking stopped. He was warm, too warm, but that warmth flooded into me and stilled my horror.

I rose slowly, helped up by this gracious brute of a man.

"My name is Tyson," he said softly. Then he turned to the rest of the bikers and shouted. "This alpha is under my protection! If she'll have me, I'll be her prime beta."

"You're my what?" I asked, voice barely there, breathy and lost.

"I'll explain everything, later," he murmured, then he turned back to the others. "Get rid of the body. You know how." He pointed to the dead man. Then he knelt and picked up my gun gingerly between two fingers, slipping it back into my purse. "Don't worry, I've got you now."

And he did too, because when I fainted, I was fairly certain I felt him catch me before I hit the ground.

TYSON

WHAT THE HELL WAS I DOING? AND HOW THE HELL HAD I ended up with this woman in my arms?

This wasn't me.

My world had been turned upside down the moment she'd killed Harley.

Before that, I'd thought her small and weak, just some silly human who was a fool for drawing the attention of our pack.

And yet... I'd never met anyone, human or wolf, who could face Harley like that. She'd been a fierce bitch protecting her pack and a part of me had respected that.

Then when she'd killed Harley... it was like some switch had been flipped inside me. For just a second my senses had been overwhelmed: blinded, deafened, numb. All I'd smelled was the sweet lavender of her perfume even though I wasn't anywhere near her. And when that inexplicable stupor had worn off, it was like she was glowing, all I could see. She'd become my entire world, and I'd had to help her, claim her, protect her.

I still didn't understand these new feelings, nor the actions they'd compelled me to perform. It went against everything I'd been taught. The commands and rules I should have followed had vanished and were replaced by a clarity and simplicity of purpose: serve her, support her, save her.

And she *definitely* needed saving.

Without my help, she'd be dead in a week.

Brick, my father, would challenge her. She'd die. And I... I had to stop that from happening. It would mean going against my own family, but I'd just told the pack I supported her, that I wished to be her prime beta just like Brick had been for Harley.

Gods, I didn't even know this woman's name.

And looking at her now, unconscious in my arms, she seemed so small and frail, yet still somehow extraordinary. Thick waves of brown hair framed a lightly tanned face, worn with lines across her forehead and at the edges of her eyes – soft brown eyes that had shone like a beacon before she'd passed out. Her cherry-red lipstick emphasized thin lips. She smelled of soap and lavender, but beneath that manufactured perfume, I caught her true scent of sun-warmed skin and the fresh aroma of dewy spring grasses. Some might think her plain, but she was the most beautiful woman I'd ever seen, perfect. I knew, without a doubt, she was *mine*.

No... *I* was *hers*.

And when her hand had touched mine a moment ago, I'd seen in her eyes that she'd felt it too, a bond between us.

"You heard the man. Get to work!" I knew that voice, the hard alto of my mom.

Instantly, the pack began to move, picking up Harley's body and taking it away. They'd dispose of it in the forest, away from prying eyes, since it was a rather gruesome process. The body would be hacked up, cleaving meat from bone. The flesh and organs would be burned to ash. The bones were kept and spread among the pack, chewed and eaten in our wolf forms, taking our former alpha's strength into us. It was how all shifters were disposed of. It was gruesome but necessary. We'd learned long ago that we couldn't leave any trace of our kind. If any scientist worth their salt got ahold of any part of us, our centuries-old secret would get out.

"Get inside, girl."

I glanced over to see my mom talking to our new alpha's daughter.

"You're not going to hurt her, are you?" the young woman asked, clearly terrified but showing strength enough to address us.

"No." The word was out before I could even process that I'd said it. "Never. And I wouldn't hurt you, little pup. Your mother and your family are under my protection now."

"Oh." The daughter blinked, confused for a long moment, then simply nodded. She backed away, then stumbled back to the house.

"What's gotten into you?" my mom hissed at me.

"I don't know!" I hissed back, still baffled by all of this. It didn't make any sense. "It's like my entire body's on fire, and the only thing that puts it out is touching her, protecting her."

"Gods damn it," my mom said with a stern look. "You sure?"

"Sure of what?" How could I be sure of something I couldn't explain?

"That that's how you feel? Burning up? You have to be near her, touch her, protect her?"

"Yeah, and I have no idea why!"

My mom's frustration mirrored my own. "Fuck," she hissed, struggling to find the right words. "This can't... you can't..."

She knew something... or at least suspected something.

"What?" I demanded, desperate for any insight. "What is this curse?"

She barked a bitter laugh, a mix of sympathy and concern in her eyes. "Curse indeed." She winced, her expression revealing that she did know more than she let on. "I can't be certain... Tell me everything."

Carrying my new alpha back to her house, I recounted the events, my mind racing, trying to make sense of it all. My mom followed, listening intently. The look on her face only got grimmer, and I could tell she knew what this was. When I finished — stopping at the front door, unsure if I should go in — I waited as my mom shook her head.

"I don't know how or why, but you've gone and gotten yourself fated to this little whelp of a woman. Fuck, Tyson, why her?"

"I don't know! What does that even mean? Fated?"

Since I'd been old enough to ride, I'd been groomed by Harley to be the next alpha. I knew everything about our kind... or so I'd thought.

I turned and sat on the front step, the woman still laying in my arms, and my mom sat next to me and put a comforting arm around my shoulders.

"It means that you're bound to her. That you're her mate, for life. That you'll do anything and everything in your power for her, to serve and protect her. It means that if she dies, you'll probably go mad. *That's* what fated means."

That certainly matched how I felt. "Fuck."

"Yeah." My mom shook her head. "Tyson, you know she'll be dead in a week. There's no way Brick or Tank won't challenge her. And now that they know she has a gun, they'll be wary. If they're shifted, bullets won't mean as much to them. They'll kill her, and you... I don't know, Tyson. This is messed up."

"I won't let them harm her," I growled, even though some part of me knew I wouldn't be able to protect her in an alpha challenge. I'd be an outcast if I did.

"You guys are werewolves, aren't you?" came the unsteady, cracking voice of a teen boy from behind me.

I looked over my shoulder at the kid that had started all of this. The pup had run out, waving at us. When we'd stopped, he'd said he knew our secret.

"Why?" I asked him, growling. "Why would you do something like that? It was foolish and dangerous. *Especially* if you know what we are."

"Cause werewolves are cool! I was hoping you'd bite me and make me strong, like you."

It was clear the little pup had watched too much TV. I glared at him, letting a partial shift take my eyes, fading from dark blue to golden yellow.

"Yeah, we're what you say, but we *won't* bite you," I growled. "We aren't superheroes. We're villains and you don't want to join us."

The kid backed off, trembling, nodding. Then ran back into the house.

I returned my eyes to their human shade and sighed.

"It's too late," my mom whispered beside me. "This woman claimed our pack, which means her pack joins ours. That kid is one of us now, even if he hasn't been bitten yet."

"Fuck," I said, yet again. She was right.

This was messed up, and there wasn't a way out of it.

I *needed* this woman to live. But that meant I had to teach her to fight... *in a week*.

Moreover, in that time, I also needed to instruct her on how to run a pack and what it meant to rule a gang of shifters. Most likely, I'd have to turn her, too.

It was a good thing the full moon was tomorrow night. That was a stroke of luck, at least. I had one week to make sure that my fated — a woman who wasn't a wolf and had no clue we existed — could fight and survive an alpha challenge with my father, who'd been a wolf his entire life.

I breathed a final, confounded, "Fuck."

We didn't have time for this woman to remain unconscious. Gods, I *really* needed to know her name. I needed to wake her and get her ready. Now.

I tapped her cheek lightly and whispered, "Wake up."

"She just killed a man. I think it'll take more than a light tap to wake her," my mom said.

"You're right." But I wasn't going to hit her any harder. I couldn't. I rose and took her inside.

The house was a bungalow with a wide front room divided into a living room, dining room, and kitchen, from left to right. I set her on a couch, then went to the kitchen, found a cup, and filled it with water. Returning, I splashed it on her face.

The woman sputtered, waking.

Time for some hard truths.

But first I knelt beside her and asked, "What's your name?"

"Jane," she said, before she'd fully come to herself. She wiped the water from her face, then looked at me, eyes going wide. "You..."

"I'm Tyson. We need to talk."

The woman's eyes rolled back and she fainted again.

This was *not* going well.

JANE

ALL I WANTED TO DO WAS STAY HERE IN THIS WARM comfortable darkness.

I'd had a horrible dream and I couldn't believe I'd been so violent. Then again, I *would* do anything to protect my family. Still, shooting someone was a stretch even for me.

Yes, I'd bought a gun, but I'd never planned on using it.

It's a deterrent. That's what I'd told myself when I'd purchased it.

So... yeah, that had all been a dream, and now I was back in the space between sleep and waking. Soon I'd wake up and have a nice normal day.

Cold wetness splashed over me... again.

I sputtered awake. That dangerous-looking but strangely kind man from my dream knelt beside my bed... no... not my bed, the couch in the living room.

It couldn't be. If he was here, that meant... it hadn't been a dream. It had all been real.

"Don't faint again, please," the man — he'd said his name was Tyson — pleaded.

"Easy for you to say. You didn't just kill a man!" I snapped at him, my words a bit slurred and my mind still foggy. My head ached, my world spinning.

"Not today, no, but I've killed before. I know it leaves a mark. Still, you don't have time to lie down. There are things you need to know."

Wait. He'd killed people before?

Who *was* this guy?

A biker... from the gang that had been terrorizing my street. And he was in my house. None of this made any sense.

I put a hand to my throbbing — and wet — forehead, closing my eyes for a moment. Blocking out the light helped lessen the pain shooting through my skull. Maybe letting him talk would get him to leave.

"Fine," I grumbled. "Talk."

I heard his grunt. He wasn't happy. Well, screw him. My day had been far worse than his.

Tyson remained silent long enough that I cracked one eyelid to peek up at him. He gazed at the floor, combing his large hand back through waves of dark hair. Squinting with only one eye like this, he sort of looked like Jason Momoa.

Finally, he sighed, his eyes shifting back to me, and I closed my one eye again to listen.

"Do you know why your son was out there this morning?" he asked slowly.

That hadn't been what I was expecting. "No. He's

always been impulsive and headstrong, but this... I thought I'd taught him better."

"Apparently not," Tyson said dryly. "Somehow your kid found out our secret."

Secret? I didn't like the sound of that. "What secret?" I asked.

"Do you believe in the paranormal?" he asked, but kept going, not waiting for an answer. "Let's start a bit easier. Do you believe in God and angels, hell and demons?"

"No." My mom had been a devout catholic and I'd gone to church as a kid, but when I'd left home, I'd left all that behind. Sundays were for shopping and laundry and cleaning.

"Ah... well... fuck."

"Just say it," I muttered, getting impatient. I didn't know where he was going and I didn't want this to drag out.

He grunted. "We're werewolves. Wolf shifters to be precise. Not all of us are wolves, but most of us are."

With everything else that had happened today, I couldn't help but laugh. Yeah... right... werewolves. The more I thought about it, the funnier it got.

"Well..." Tyson said, laughing a little with me. "That's better than the usual reaction." Then he sighed. "But I don't think you believe me. So..." There was a long silence, though I did hear what sounded like the rustling of cloth. After that... I heard the strangest sound: creepy and awful, like someone cracking their knuckles, if they had a thousand knuckles.

"Open your eyes." I could barely understand his words, they were slurred and awkward.

I didn't want to open my eyes. If I didn't, then I could remain in my own quiet oblivion a little longer. But if I did... I knew what I'd see. He was going to show me proof of his claim and I just... couldn't... that wasn't...

I peeked open one eyelid again... seeing only a fur-covered leg where his head had been. I slammed that lid shut quickly.

Nope, definitely not opening them anymore. Were-wolves weren't real. This wasn't happening. This had to be some terrible dream. If I just waited, I'd wake up and get dressed and go to work.

Work.

Fuck!

If this wasn't a dream, I was going to be horribly late for work! It was an hour's drive to Reston, and that was assuming traffic wasn't horrible on the 267. But... no, this was a dream it had to be. Please God, let it be a dream!

"We don't have time for this!" a woman said, voice low and gravelly. Then someone slapped my face, startling me. The act was immediately followed by a growl, a very inhuman growl.

"Mom! Don't!" These words were slurred like the ones before.

Mom?

I opened my eyes, confused and alarmed.

Sitting on the couch next to me was a tough-looking woman in biker's leathers, and next to her... was a monster.

I screamed, scrambling away, climbing the arm of the

couch and sitting there with my back to the front window.

The beast seemed to be half man and half wolf. The head was all wolf, but the body had the rough figure of a man, just... covered in fur. It stood on two legs, but the legs were bent all wrong. What really caught my attention were the claws on its massive hands, and the fangs in that canine mouth. That and the size. The beast was huge. I couldn't stop screaming.

Behind the creature, Izzy and Milo hurried out from the back hall to see what had shocked me. Izzy's eyes went wide and she screamed.

Milo grinned and shouted, "I knew it!"

For some reason that made me stop screaming. My thirteen-year-old son wasn't scared at all?

The creature shifted and seemed to collapse in on itself. That horrid noise of popping bones returned, making me shiver in revulsion. A moment later, in the beast's place, was Tyson, a very well-muscled and very naked man.

"Believe me now?" he asked.

I couldn't stop staring at him. A part of my brain couldn't register what it had just seen. It had to have been a delusion. Yet, another part *did* believe. And that belief was shattering everything I knew about the world.

A third part of my brain — a part that hadn't had sex in ten years, since my ex-husband had left me — made my eyes roam over that incredibly sexy body.

Tyson was a *very* handsome man. I didn't usually go for tattoos, but his bad boy look made him seem all the sexier, forbidden and dangerous. And when my eyes inevitably dipped down...

Wow! Even limp that dick was like something out of a fantasy... or porn.

Tyson didn't seem to care that he was naked in my living room as he took his time putting his clothes back on.

It was Milo who broke the heavy silence which had settled over all of us. "I knew it! That's so cool! Hey Mom, can I be a werewol—?"

"No!" Tyson and I shouted at the same time.

Milo huffed and pouted. "Fine." Then he slunk back to his room.

Izzy was still staring at Tyson. I couldn't blame her. He'd been a monster just a moment ago. Also, he was incredibly swoonworthy. He'd put on jeans, but that still left a slab of chest with chiseled abs and arms rippling with muscles that shifted and flexed as he pulled on his shirt.

"Mom?" Izzy whispered. "What...?"

I wished I could answer.

It was the other woman in the room who did. "You're part of our pack now, little pup. Your mother killed our alpha and rules us now. You're gonna have to get used to it." The woman's hard gaze landed on me. "That's assuming your mother gets her act together and wolf's up in a week's time."

Izzy, eyes glazed over, mouth gaping, nodded slowly and turned then wordlessly walked back to her room.

I still couldn't speak.

"I know I scared you," Tyson said softly, "but I'll never

hurt you. Yes, we're werewolves, but I've sworn myself to you. I'll protect you. You don't need to fear me."

The other woman scoffed. "I don't think she believes you." Her gaze held mine for a moment. "But she will." She stood. "She will when she sees the rest of the pack testing her and realizes you're the only one on her side. And that's going to start happening real soon, lady. So, you'd better get your act together."

"Wh-who are you?" I managed to stammer. It was partly a question to find out who this woman was, but mostly a general question to the world about these beings.

"Name's Kira," the woman said. "I'm Tyson's mother."

Right. He'd mentioned that.

"Mother?" I repeated, mostly because that was a word I knew and it seemed easy to say. My brain just wasn't ready to take this all in.

But Kira snarled and slapped me... hard.

"Mom!" Tyson's tone turned threatening and he grabbed her wrist. "I warned you. I won't let you hurt her. Don't make me hurt *you*. I *have* to protect her!" his voice was strained.

Between his reaction and those words... I was beginning to believe it. This monster, or whatever-the-hell he was, wanted to help me, protect me.

"Why?" I asked, turning my gaze to him.

"I'm fated for you," he said softly.

I huffed. I had no clue what that meant, and something in how he'd said it made me believe he didn't really know either.

"As soon as you became alpha, I felt it. A compulsion

to protect you, to—" Something in those dark blue eyes flared. I felt completely naked before him. Then he blinked and the moment passed. "To help you, serve you."

"Oh," I whispered. That was... interesting.

"He also wants to fuck you. That's what he didn't say," Kira said, voice hard. "He's compelled to be with you, in all senses of the word." She smiled at my wide eyes and Tyson's threatening glare. "What? Better to tell her the truth now. It's not like we have the benefit of time."

"Why not?" I asked. I was slowly starting to regain myself and it was clear these two were very keen to make sure I understood things *immediately*.

"Because in a few minutes the pack is going to return," Tyson answered. "They're going to take up residence here, in your house, and they'll be expecting you to lead them. They'll test you far more than teenagers probing their boundaries. And if you aren't the alpha they want, then in seven days, one of them will challenge you and probably kill you. That's why."

I felt the faintness and darkness returning, my body weakening.

I quickly slapped myself to stay conscious. These two were right. I didn't have time to faint.

"All right," I said, my voice trembling, my mind barely believing any of what they were saying. "Tell me everything."

JANE

"WANT COFFEE?" TYSON ASKED. "MAYBE SOMETHING stronger? This isn't going to be easy or quick. Might as well fortify yourself."

Outside, I heard the school bus stopping at the end of our street.

Bus.

School.

The kids!

"Kids, the bus is here. You need to go!" I called out on instinct.

"Something tells me they'll be taking a sick day," Tyson said. "They'll need to get up to speed quickly as well. And wherever you were going today, call in sick. In fact, call in sick for the next week. You don't have time to be anywhere but here."

"Yeah," I said as that sunk in.

Izzy and Milo came out from the back.

"School?" Milo asked while Izzy wore a stunned

expression, her eyes darting around, probably looking for more monsters.

"No," I said. "I changed my mind. I'll call the school and tell them you're sick. Have a seat, this nice man is going to explain some things to us." As I said this, I got up, grabbed my purse and pulled out my phone. I had their schools on speed dial. I called Milo's first, then Izzy's, quickly telling the receptionists who answered they wouldn't be in.

While I did that, I went into the kitchen and started the coffee maker. Usually, I picked up coffee-to-go on the way to work, but that wouldn't be happening today. As I waited for that to brew, I got out a bottle of wine and a glass. I filled it to the rim then gulped it back. That didn't do much. By the end of the second glass, my mind was easing just a little.

Good.

"Time to talk," I said. "Where did the others go and when will they be back?"

Kira looked at Tyson, who sighed. "They've gone to dispose of Harley's body. It's... not a quick or nice process, but it means science hasn't discovered that we exist. It's horrible, but effective." Now I didn't want to know. "They'll probably be an hour or so," he finished.

"Then talk. Let's hear it. Everything. Go."

I leaned against the kitchen counter. Kira leaned against the front door. Tyson took a seat at the dining room table between me in the kitchen and my kids, who were stiffly sitting in the living room.

Tyson blew out a breath. "Where to start? How about

a bit of history? Sure. So... everything you know about the world is probably wrong. All those things you dismissed as nonsense, supernatural, or religious hype, yeah, they're all real. Demons, angels, and gods? All real. Also, witches and magic."

Gods? As in... plural?

But before I could ask about that, Milo shouted out, "And dragons?"

"Yeah, they're out there. Though as far as I know, no one's seen one in a while."

"Cool!" Milo crooned, a big grin on his face.

Tyson laughed, then went on, "Yeah, so all of that is real. I know it doesn't mean much just to hear someone say it, but—"

"Do witches like to dance around naked?" Milo asked.

I frowned at him. Where had that come from?

"Yeah... sometimes, why?" Tyson asked.

Milo suddenly blushed furiously. "Ah... no reason, keep going."

My frown deepened. I knew that face. My boy had seen something, but now wasn't the time to find out what.

"Go on," I prompted Tyson. I knew I had to believe him, but still, I was having a hard time with all this.

"So yeah, pretty much any mythical thing you've heard of probably exists, or did exist a long time ago." Tyson's voice was gentle, trying to ease me into the reality of their world. "Which brings us to werewolves. The thing you need to know about what we are is... it's a curse."

I listened intently, but the words felt like a heavy

weight pressing down on my chest. I couldn't believe what I was hearing.

"Thousands of years ago, wild men put on the pelts of wolves and hunted other men, eating their flesh. They justified this cannibalism saying they were overcome with the nature of the beast while wearing the skins of wolves. So, the Archangel Michael cursed those men to become true wolves, losing their humanity. Some were eventually able to change themselves back... and that's how this all began. Now, it's a blood-borne virus that *can* be transmitted through a bite, but, contrary to popular belief, that isn't one hundred percent effective. To be sure, you need to exchange blood. It's also transmissible through sex."

Tyson's gaze briefly met mine, and I could feel the intensity of his emotions, a longing that both intrigued and scared me. His mother had said part of being 'fated' meant he'd want to fuck me, and an aching part of me wanted him to. But if he did... I'd become a werewolf, so that was off the table.

"Also, we're not the only kind of shifter. Others have been cursed in a similar way. Tank, the big guy from our pack, is a bear shifter, and there are a couple other bears in our pack as well. We also have a lion shifter." Tyson's gaze drifted up to meet mine. "We're not good people. We do horrible things. We're cursed and... most of us like it that way." His jaw tensed for a moment. "And I'm sorry Jane, but you're going to have to become one of us if you want to survive."

I swallowed hard, turning away. I made a show of

pouring the coffee, but really, I just needed a moment. I trembled. Some distant part of me had guessed that's where this was all going, but still.... I didn't want to be cursed. I didn't want any of this.

But I had no choice now.

If I wanted to protect my family and survive, I'd have to accept it.

"And my kids?" I asked, unable to keep my voice from quavering.

"They don't *need* to, but they're a part of the pack now and it'll be awkward if they aren't turned. Just the slightest mishap could turn them. It doesn't take much blood at all."

I shook so badly I couldn't pick up my mug. I'd slosh the black liquid everywhere. I leaned on the counter, clamping my hands around the fringe at the sink.

"No." My voice was as firm as I could make it. "I may have to do this, but they don't. I'll keep them safe."

"Then so will I," Tyson said stoically behind me.

"Aw... Mom!" Milo whined. I ignored him.

Tyson's reassurance allowed me to regain some measure of control. I didn't know this man at all, but he'd made it very clear he was here for me, whatever I needed, and I had a feeling I was going to need him a lot in the days to come.

I picked up my coffee and turned back, taking a sip.

That lapse in control a moment ago only highlighted how well I was keeping my shit together. A part of me wanted to scream that this was insane, but I was nothing if not pragmatic. I'd always worked hard and pushed through difficult times, no stranger to struggle. I was the only female manager at my accounting firm, and I'd had to work three times as hard as any man to get there. I should have been an executive, but the boys club at the top would never let that happen. Still, I'd done well for myself, and provided a decent life for my kids.

Now all of that was in danger. I couldn't let that happen. I had to take control.

"So, how do I run a pack of biker werewolves?" I asked directly.

Tyson sighed. "That's the problem. For most of them... all they've ever known is brute force and violence. They've been kept in their place by someone stronger or tougher or more dangerous all their lives. Some of the pack are younger or newer and won't be as hard to control, but..."

"You're going to have trouble with the old betas," Kira said, voice cold. "That's Tank, Sonny, and Brick. Brick also happens to be my husband, even if I hate the bastard."

Her husband? Wow.

I recalled the three older, rough-looking men who'd been backing the leader.

"Brick is also my father," Tyson added.

I gaped. If my mind had actually been working at full capacity, I'd have recalled he'd called Kira his mother... which would make Brick his father. As it was, I just couldn't reconcile the seemingly kind man before me with the brute I'd met earlier.

"The other one you'll probably have trouble with is Ginny." Tyson sighed. "She was Harley's girl and had a lot of power because of it. Now she's got nothing and will probably resent you for that," Tyson said, matter-of-factly.

"Any others?" I asked. Better to know now.

Tyson began to list off names, most of them meant nothing to me. "Bronn and Colt are loyal to me, I can bring them to our side. Rita and Brutus, my sister and brother, I can probably win over. They don't care much for our father. Rita is a tough nut though and plays things close to the chest, so... I don't know. Brutus would rather be a wolf, so if you let him do that, he'll probably be fine. The Juarez family are decent people, they could be convinced to join us, I think. So too with Cassie and her kid."

I did the math. That was at least eight, depending on how big the 'Juarez family' was.

But... "You didn't include your mother in that count." I looked at Kira. "Are you going to be trouble?"

Her hard steel-blue eyes matched my look. Then she smiled, even if it was a hard smile.

"My kids have always been everything to me." She didn't look away as her expression turned sour. "When I was young, I actually liked Brick and the power he possessed. I was just like him. Then I had Rita and everything changed. Brick didn't care one bit for our kids, but I... I knew I had to protect them. Over the years, my desire to keep the kids safe drove a wedge between Brick and me. Eventually I came to see all the kids in the pack as mine. I tried to smooth over the harsh realities of our life as much as I could."

Her jaw twitched as she looked at Tyson. There was something in that look — something I felt viscerally as a mother — a sense of failure in her sacred duty. With a deep breath, her gaze swung back at me.

"Now, I have two more kids to take care of," she said, looking at Izzy and Milo. "If you let me help mother them, I'll have your back. That's all I want."

Good. I'd probably need someone watching them if I was going to have my hands full with a pack of wolves. "Thank you," I said earnestly. "I'd appreciate that." I looked at Tyson. "Anyone else?"

"Petra and Winnie. If you can keep them away from Tank and Sonny respectively, you'll probably earn their undying gratitude, but that won't be easy. Petra is pregnant with Tank's kid and Winnie is Sonny's daughter and needs to act loyal to him no matter how she may feel."

Wow, this pack was truly messed up.

And that's when it sank in. They *were* messed up... and they were *my* problem now.

"Fu—" With my kids in the room I didn't want to swear. "—n"

From the sounds of it, there were more women in the group than I'd expected. I'd not really taken a good look at the bikers when they'd passed by and I'd assumed most of them were men. It sounded like roughly half were women. Interesting.

"So..." I went through the list again in my head. "It sounds like only four will be a problem?"

Tyson sighed. "Yeah, but... that's the thing. Those four are used to bossing around the rest, and the rest are used to being bossed around by them. Without them on board, they'll keep trying to assert control over the others."

"Okay, so how do I get them on board. Is that possible?"

Tyson shook his head. "I don't think so. They were loyal to Harley and you killed him. They're going to hate you for that."

"Great."

"Sonny *might* be convinced," Kira said, but she didn't sound hopeful. "Of the three betas he was the last to come along and the least aggressive." She shook her head. "But still, Harley was good to him. It would take something close to a miracle to get him to forget Harley."

"So... what do I do?" I asked. This sounded impossible.

Tyson looked over at his mother and she nodded at him. Something in him strengthened in that moment and his voice was resolved when he spoke next.

"I was next in line to rule the pack," he said slowly. "Harley had no kids of his own and was grooming me to be the next alpha. I might be able to keep Tank, Sonny, and Brick at bay while you try to pull the others away and run the pack your way. And I'll have help. Bronn and Colt were to be my betas. I could probably convince them to join me as your betas, if you'll have them. That would be even more of a buffer between you and the previous betas."

"My pack, my way? What does that mean?" I asked, confused.

It was Kira who answered. "You haven't been brought up in this life. It's rough and it makes people hard. If you try to be an alpha like Harley, you'll fail." She looked me over with detached appraisal. "You're too soft. There's no way we can make you hard enough in one week. So play to your strengths. Be yourself. Be the leader *you* want to be. Hopefully the pack will want what you're offering."

"And what do you think I'm offering?" I asked her.

"A life without needing to be hard all the time, without fear of reprisal because of some minor slight. You'll still need to have mettle in your bones if you're going to do this, but if you show them they can have a different way of life, I think most would want that."

"And you?" I asked her directly. "Do you want that?"

She hedged, humming and hawing, the first hint of awkwardness I'd seen from her. Eventually she said, "I'm fifty-five years old."

I raised my brows. She didn't look a day over my own age of forty-four.

"I've lived this way all my life," she continued. "I don't know how easy it would be for me to change."

"Ah," I said, surprisingly disappointed.

"But..." She drew out the word. "Like I said. I do this for the kids. And I've seen too many kids made hard far too early. It might be nice to get to see some pups grow up without fearing their alpha." She laughed. "I just have no clue what that looks like."

Wow. I couldn't imagine what she might have seen. It sounded horrible. I swore I wouldn't be that sort of alpha. My kids knew their boundaries — or so I hoped — but I didn't think they feared me. They just knew that certain actions had consequences.

I sighed and made my way over to the dining room table to sit with Tyson. "You really think we can do this? That *I* can do this?"

"Yeah," he said softly. "But I'm going to have to turn you into one of us, and soon. Luckily, the full moon is tomorrow. You'll have your first shift then and it's not going to be nice. But after that, you can start to understand what we go through. That will give you five more days to figure shit out."

The thought of being 'turned' terrified me, but I nodded in agreement. I got the feeling that part wasn't negotiable. If I was going to run a wolf pack... I'd need to be a wolf.

"And how do we do the... turning part?" I asked.

"Didn't you hear him, Mom?" Milo burst out. "Blood to blood." He sounded far too eager.

"Or..." Izzy said with a hint of mischief in her voice. "Sex."

Tyson's gaze never left mine. His dark blue eyes devoured me with primal lust. An overwhelming heat filled my chest, then sank into my core. He didn't have to say which would be his preferred option. I could see it in his eyes.

Then he whispered, "Blood to blood will work."

A part of me was so very thankful for that.

Another part... extremely disappointed.

"Okay." I drew in a long breath as Tyson's gaze shifted away and I was suddenly left feeling bereft and cold. "So, how do we do this?"

We discussed our plans before the others returned. Tyson and his friends, Bronn and Colt, would run interference between myself and the old betas. Kira would help. She had enough power as a beta's wife to stand up to them. Meanwhile, I'd work my... charm... on the rest of the pack and try to win them over to my side. I just had to figure out what my side actually was. Because if my proposal wasn't tempting enough, it wouldn't overcome the packs fear of the old betas.

But before I had time to start thinking about that, the others began to arrive.

BRONN

I KNEW THE DEATH RITUAL WELL ENOUGH, BUT IT STILL sickened me. So, I'd been quite happy that the pack left me out when Harley's bones were passed around. That was Brick's doing. He'd never liked me, and he loved to show the pack just how much he didn't like me.

Of the many scars on my body, some had come from Harley, some from Tank, but most were from Brick. The wolf beta glared at me as he gnawed on his previous alpha's bones. It was customary to do so in animal form, since humans eating bones was barbaric. But Brick was barbaric enough to skirt that custom. He raked the sinew and blood off the bones with his teeth and seemed to like it. It made me want to vomit, but I couldn't leave, not until this little ceremony was done. The rest of the pack, as wolves, were in a rough circle chewing on the bones of their former leader, breaking them down slowly. It wasn't a quick process. They'd take the bones with them and continue to work on them over the next few weeks.

Brick broke the large leg bone with a sickening crack

and began sucking out the marrow. I held back bile, which burned in my throat.

Then finally, Brick called to the others and they shifted back. The bones were hidden away, the pack dressed and we got on our bikes.

"We'll take the bikes for a spin before we park them, tear up that nice lawn and garden of hers," Brick said with a laugh as we made our way back to the woman's house. "Then make sure to stomp around in the mud before we go in, wreck her carpet. Let's just see her try to stop us, that should be a laugh."

Sonny gave a snort.

"We'll ruin her house and her life," Tank said, viciously. I knew the man well enough to know he was furious. The lecherous bear shifter had wanted to rape that woman, but now that she was alpha, she was off limits. So, he'd just cause her as much grief as he could. "Then in a week, I'll tear her a new one."

"You'll do nothing of the sort," Brick said, putting Tank in his place. "She's mine. I'll be the next alpha, now that my son has lost his mind. I can't believe that whelp protected her! I don't know what he was thinking, but if he's her beta, he's no son of mine. He was supposed to be an alpha, not a beta. Fucking stupid little shit."

I couldn't understand what had come over Tyson either. Of the entire pack, Tyson had been the only one to ever treat me with any respect. As the next alpha, groomed to lead, he was supposed to make his own decisions, and when he'd taken me under his wing, mostly protecting me from his father's attacks, I'd become forever loyal to him.

I'd been taken from my father's pride — the Kings — when I was sixteen. The Fangs — Harley's pack, which now belonged to that enigmatic woman — had defeated The Kings in a turf war in Morgantown. The price had been the disbanding of my father's MC. The Fangs took their bikes — selling most of them — and myself as their prize. I'd been a mouthy and cocky young lion shifter back then and I'd earned myself a lot of beatings after I'd been branded as a wolf. One on one, I could take any wolf, but in a pack, I had no chance. I'd learned to keep my mouth shut and take any punishment — deserving or not — they dealt me.

Then Tyson had claimed me. I hadn't known much about the young man back then, but I'd quickly learned he was tough and could stand up to his father... and often did on my behalf. If he was serving that woman now... then I'd follow him and serve her too. The fact that Brick was against it made it all the more appealing.

Still, dread roiled in my gut at the thought of going against the old betas. Years of abuse and beatings had left their toll on me. I'd learned not to show my hatred, not to talk back or show any sign of a backbone. But now...?

We reached the woman's house. The others went for their bikes. I left mine at the side of the street and headed for the front door.

"Hey, pussy, get back here!" Tank called. That was his favorite nickname for me. For a moment I froze, years of instincts kicking in. I should obey...

"Go fuck yourself, Dad," Colt called as he stepped up next to me, putting a thick arm around my shoulders.

"Don't listen to him," Colt whispered. "We know who we serve."

I smiled and nodded, allowing myself to relax a bit. Colt was an odd one, but I knew I could trust him. He might be Tank's son, and just as big as his father — with a baby-face and a cheery smile — but he was loyal to Tyson. His father had stopped beating him once Colt had been large enough to fight back. Not long after that, he too had been brought into Tyson's little band. Colt and I would have been Tyson's betas if he'd become alpha... now...?

"Get back here, whelps!" Brick shouted.

"Not gonna happen," Colt whispered. It seemed even Colt wasn't stupid enough to counter Brick out loud. As much as Tank was a beast, Brick was the real power behind this pack now.

The two of us continued into the house. Once there, we'd be safe enough... assuming Tyson was there.

I pushed on the front door, which didn't open. There was resistance, probably someone leaning on the door. The muffled voices on the other side stopped their conversation and a moment later Kira opened the door.

"Get in here!" she hissed, glancing outside with an assessing look. She closed the door behind us, then turned to the woman, our new alpha. "I hope you don't much care for your lawn, I think the boys are gonna tear it up."

"They are," I said. "Then they're going to track all the mud from that mess in here."

Kira laughed. "Yeah right, they'll have to go through

me first. I'll see to it this place remains mostly intact. We're going to be living here, after all."

Our new alpha shook her head, a hard look on her face. This was the first good look I'd had of the woman and I was just a bit stunned at how lovely she was.

Sure, there wasn't anything exotic about her, but that fall of wavy brown hair and her mostly smooth, fair skin painted a picture of mature beauty. She had large, dark, caramel-brown eyes and a body of womanly curves, but it was her scent that truly captured me.

Lions identified each other by scent. It was also how we chose our mates, and this woman's scent called to me. The smell of lavender soap, which wafted around her, wasn't unpleasant, but her true scent was far more alluring. She smelled of spring, of sweet dewy grasses and sun-warmed skin. I'd never smelled anything more like *home* in my life.

I knelt before her. "Alpha, I am yours to command," I said, hoping with my entire being she'd be different than Harley. She had to be... didn't she?

"Ah... yeah, me too," Colt said beside me.

"Get up, you fuckers," Tyson said playfully. I stood as he introduced us. "Jane, this is Bronn and Colt." He indicated the two of us. "They're with me." Then to us. "Bronn, Colt, this is Jane, our new alpha." He hiked a thumb over his shoulder. "Over there are her kids, Izzy and Milo."

I hadn't even noticed the two cubs in the living room. The boy was the one who'd run out calling to us, saying he knew our secret. That one wasn't going to last long if he kept up that level of idiocy. And the girl... I didn't know how old she was, only that we'd have to keep her away from Tank.

Tyson sighed, drawing my attention back to him. "And *here's* something interesting, Jane is my fated mate. So yeah, we have to make sure she stays alive after a week's up or I'll probably go mad."

I blinked. "What? Fuck no!" Suddenly all my fears returned in a tidal wave. "Tyson, if you go..." Then I'd have nothing to protect me from the betas and whoever the new alpha was... probably Brick.

"Shit," Colt drew out the word. "That's fucked up."

The roar of bike engines outside caused all of us to speak louder as we continued.

"Which means I need you three to help me," Jane said.

I was surprised at the rigid determination in her voice. This couldn't be easy for her. She wasn't a shifter. I had no clue how she was holding up so well. It made me respect her all the more.

"I have a plan for how to get through the next week," she said, "But I'm going to need as much help as I can get convincing the pack my way is better than what they've known their entire life, while also learning to protect myself and fight as a wolf." She bit her lip for a moment. Even just that little sign of uncertainty was very un-alpha-like. When she spoke again it was asking, not demanding, also very un-alpha-like. "And could you please stop swearing so much in front of my children?"

Colt laughed. "Sorry, alpha, we're rough-as-they-come bikers. We three might be able to hold our tongues, but the others aren't going to be so kind. I think your kids are just gonna get an education in cussing."

She sighed, so... demure. It was baffling and alluring all at the same time. I wanted to hold her, ease her cares away. It was a beta's duty to look after their alpha, after all. But that hadn't really been formalized yet, had it?

"Have you chosen your betas?" I asked. I'd assumed we'd be her betas because of our bond to Tyson, but...

Jane blinked. She looked at Tyson. "You'd said these two would be my beta's too, right?"

He nodded. "An alpha needs to officially claim his... ah... or *her* betas."

"How do I do that?" she asked with a glance at Colt and myself. Something in that look suggested she was truly seeing us for the first time. "Oh... you're... big men, aren't you? So young and strapping and... ah..." She blew out a breath, a blush on her cheeks, which only enhanced her beauty.

"There is no formal or right way. Some alphas fight and find the strongest of the pack to be their betas, others simply say the words and make it so. Most of the time an alpha knows who is closest to him in the pack and chooses them as his betas. But for you..." Tyson shrugged. "What feels right to you?"

She took a moment, her pink tongue darting out to wet her lips. I knew it was just lipstick but the cherry-red shade she'd chosen set off her mostly fair, slightly tanned complexion perfectly.

She bit her lip again and it made me want to bite into that soft, red fullness. "I..."

She swallowed heavily, drawing my attention to her

long, elegant neck. I wanted to bite there too, not hard, just rake my teeth over her soft skin. I wouldn't truly bite her. Going for the throat was a sign of dominance to my cat instincts. If anything, as my alpha, she should be biting my neck, and a part of me really wanted her to. But she wasn't even a shifter and... all of this was just a strange, confusing mess. Yet, a mess I wanted to dive fully into.

"Can I kiss you?" she asked hesitantly.

Tyson cocked his head. "I knew it. You felt it too, when we touched?"

"I felt your warmth. It seemed to fill me and calm me and..." She swallowed again. "I know it sounds forward, but I can't explain it. I just want to..."

Kira broke the moment. "It's the fated bond. It'll make you wanna fuck like bunnies. You may not be there yet, but you're starting to feel it. Once you become a wolf it'll be stronger and when you're in heat it'll be nearly impossible to resist."

"In heat?" Jane's eyes went wide. "That happens?"

Kira gave a sour smile. "How else do you think I ended up with three kids from a bastard of a man."

"Are you fated too?" Jane asked the older woman.

"Hell no! But the heat still affects non-fated females."

"Oh."

The bikes were starting to quiet outside.

"If you want any privacy, you'd better claim us now," Tyson said, and I heard the expectant pull of his voice. He wanted to feel the touch of her lips as much as I did.

"You two, get to your rooms, now!" Kira said from

behind me, telling Jane's cubs to scram before the pack arrived.

Jane rose from behind the dining table. Tyson got up as well and we came to her in turns. Tyson, of course, went first. Jane may have been a bit taller than average, but Tyson still towered over her. He bent down, taking her face in both hands as she tilted her head back to meet his lips.

The kiss was soft... for a moment, then something inside both of them seemed to break and they both pushed in, opening, heavy breaths escaping from the sides of their merged lips. It looked like it took an extreme effort for Tyson to pull back, both of them breathing hard.

"Later," he whispered, to a flushed and trembling Jane.

"Promise." It wasn't a question. It was her promise to him that they'd pick that up later.

She turned to me, her chest still heaving, full bust straining against the sheer fabric of her blouse. Yet that didn't captivate me as much as her eyes. I lost myself in those large caramel-brown depths.

I wasn't as tall as Tyson, so neither of us had to bend too far to find each other's lips. She closed her eyes, head back, lips poised. I took in that submissive posture for just a moment before I dipped down to press my lips against her soft, smooth ones. We weren't fated. I didn't know how *she* felt, but I'd already lost myself in this woman. She seemed to be a confounding set of contra-dictions: soft but hard, vulnerable but determined, weak of body but strong in will, tentative but confident. I didn't understand her, not yet, but I knew, in my soul, I *needed* her.

Her arms slid around my neck, pulling me down. I couldn't help myself. I surrounded her body in my strong embrace. My lips left hers and I kissed her throat, over her pulse. She let out a soft breathy moan, spiking my arousal. Then she kissed my neck and it was nearly too much for me.

I lifted away to whisper, "your teeth," and she opened her mouth, raking her teeth over my throat in a mock bite.

My turn to gasp. I shuddered with soul-gripping submission. Her scent told me we belonged together and now her bite — even if it hadn't been a true bite — had claimed me. I was hers, now and forever. My mate. My cock was instantly rock hard and ready, just in case she wished to have me now.

I blinked away those thoughts. She wouldn't be thinking like a cat. She may not even know what she'd just done. It was torture to step back from her, but I wouldn't force myself on her. Also, she was fated to Tyson and I wouldn't get in the middle of that. Not unless both of them wanted me there.

Jane smiled, blinking up at me, with a breathy, "wow." Then she drew a long breath before moving on to Colt. He was a mountain of a man, even taller than Tyson. He bent low while Jane tilted her head all the way back and they met in the middle. The young buck's kiss was hard and playful, like the man himself.

But I was only peripherally aware of her kiss with the large man. My thoughts were still tumbling around in my head. I'd never thought I'd have a mate. I was a lion in a pack of wolves. There wasn't anyone here who'd want me. But this woman, this perfect creature... I had to have her, had to give myself to her. I'd do anything for her.

My heart thundered with the strength of my commitment. Yet still, I knew my dedication could only go as far as serving her. As Tyson's fated, she wasn't for me. I hoped I could live with that.

Jane and Colt broke apart as the front door slammed open.

Jane stepped back, adjusting herself, flushed and flustered.

"Take off your fucking boots. Now!" Kira roared at those coming in.

And so, it began.

COLT

I CLENCHED AND UNCLENCHED MY FIST BEHIND MY BACK. I didn't want Jane to see how frustrated I was. I could have killed whoever had come in and interrupted our glorious kiss.

I hardly knew this woman, but right now, I knew enough. I knew her lips were soft and her face angelic. I knew her scent of lush spring grass and sun-on-skin stirred something deep within me. I knew she was ready to fight against overwhelming odds to survive. I could see her iron will, hidden behind uncertainty and terror. And it was plain as day to me that she was fated for Tyson.

The two of them were perfect for each other. Tyson had always dreaded the thought of finding a mate. It was why he was in his mid-thirties and still without one. Harley had tried for a long time to get Tyson to mate with Sonny's daughter Winnie.

She'd been twelve when Harley had first suggested it. She'd had her first period and that was all Harley had needed. In private, Tyson had been disgusted. Publicly, he'd told Harley he wanted a woman, not a girl, and said he'd wait until she was twenty. He'd hoped he'd find his true mate in that time. But Tyson's time had been running out. Winnie was almost twenty now, but she was still a girl in too many ways. Whereas Tyson had had to grow up far too fast.

Groomed to be the next alpha, he was mature and hard, ready to rule. He needed a strong woman who could match him.

Jane was certainly all woman, mature and beautiful. And from the lack of a guy around, I guessed she was a single mother who'd raised two kids. She seemed the perfect mix of hard and soft, discipline and dedication. If so, she'd be a good match for Tyson.

The trouble was, her lips had tasted so perfectly sweet, and the press of her body to mine had thrilled me in a way I hadn't felt...

... since Tasha.

Everything about Jane sung to my soul. Breaking down the walls I'd built after Tasha's death.

And she may be fated for Tyson, but something in her kiss had opened a door and allowed me to hope that *maybe* she'd be open to being with other men in addition to her fated.

But I had to curb my fantasies about fulfilling this woman's every desire and focus on my pack at the moment.

I turned to see them piling into Jane's living room. Brick and Tank wore heavy, frustrated expressions, having been forced to remove their riding boots. I'd heard the shouting match as Brick and Kira had locked horns.

Brick would have won if Kira hadn't been acting on behalf of the alpha. He had to obey or risk punishment. We'd won a tiny victory, but there was still a lot of the war left to fight.

The others didn't seem to mind or care that they'd had to remove their boots. With everyone inside, the open concept front area of the house was suddenly crowded.

There were seventeen of us left in the pack. I could remember when we'd been twice that number. Some had been killed by rival gangs. Some had fled from Harley's brutality: a few had been found and executed, others managed to get away. Some had been killed by Harley himself, who'd taken out anyone who might challenge him, all while grooming Tyson to be his perfect heir. I found it just a little funny that Harley had been killed by some unknown suburban woman. He'd never seen that coming. None of us had.

Another point for Jane.

Brick claimed a loveseat, spreading out to take up the entire space. Sonny took one of the chairs. Tank, my brute of a father, threw himself down on one of the couches, probably trying to break it with his bulk. The furniture survived his assault, this time. Petra — my father's current lover and only three years older than me — squealed as Tank grabbed her arm and pulled her down on top of him. He reached one hand up under her shirt to fondle her roughly, while his other hand fisted her hair and drove her mouth to his, stopping any sounds of surprise or protest she might emit. Gods, I hated that man.

The rest of the pack milled about, uncertain where to go or what to do.

"Hey, bitch!" Brick called out and silenced everyone.

Among our kind, every female wolf was a bitch, but he wasn't saying it like that. He put as much hatred and vulgar insinuation into the word as he could. "Nice place, where do I sleep? I better have a bed as my station deserves!" Brick had been prime beta, and VP of the Fangs motorcycle club.

"Hell yeah, me too," Tank called out. "I can't wait to have a real mattress beneath me, or rather, beneath my girl here while I fuck her. I wonder how long it will last before I break it."

Tyson eyed me and Bronn. This was it, our time to step up. "You'll take whatever your given, Brick," Tyson said evenly. "Whatever our new alpha sees fit to give you. You're no longer a beta anymore. I'm prime beta now and you'll defer to me."

Brick rose, eyes flaring with rage. "You listen here, whelp. I ain't taking orders from you. I'll—"

"Then you'll sleep outside," Jane shouted from behind me. She'd used that special mom-voice that Kira broke out from time to time, the kind that said, "*I've-had-enough-of-your-shit*." Jane stepped between Bronn and me. "Go. Now!" She pointed toward the back of the house.

Brick took a step forward. "I'll tear your throat out, bitch!"

Bronn and I instinctively blocked his path to her, even

while she said, "I don't think you can, not for one week, isn't that right? And until then, it's clear to me, you're not house trained yet, so you sleep outside until you can act appropriately in here."

I almost laughed at the clear slapdown Jane had just given, and the outrage on Brick's face. He snarled and the shimmer of a pre-shift slid over his features before he got control of himself.

"I can't touch you... but..." He slammed his fist down on the coffee table in the living room, shattering the wood. "I can touch anything else I want."

To prove his point, he stalked over to Cassie — one of the newer members of our pack — and gave her a hard backhand slap, which sent her to the ground. She yelped then whimpered in pain. Tyson moved, pushing through the pack to get to her and help her up. Brick stared daggers at Jane.

"Every time you command me," he said, "I'll hurt someone else, just like that, because I can, because I'm going to rip your throat out and rule this pack in a week." Then he left, stalking down the back hall and crashing out the back door.

And there it was. The first of many confrontations to come, and it hadn't gone well for us.

Tank laughed, drawing our attention. He had Petra's neck in his huge hand, easily lifting her off his lap. The poor woman didn't even struggle, she'd learned the hard way not to defy Tank. Just like I'd learned... over and over... as a kid. I also knew just how willing Tank was to kill, though I was pretty sure this was a bluff. Petra was pregnant, and I was fairly certain he wanted her to have his kid. But with Tank, you never quite knew. He was truly savage. He'd killed Tasha, the woman I'd loved, and laughed while doing it. Yet another reason for me to hate him. He raised his chin defiantly at Jane.

"You gonna force me out too?" His gaze moved from Jane to Petra and back.

We weren't touching and I wasn't looking at her, but I could feel Jane's outrage, like a fire warming my side. Yet her voice was restrained when she asked. "Tyson, what's the penalty when one of *my* pack kills another of *my* pack?" I loved how easily she'd claimed all of us.

More points for Jane.

Tyson helped Cassie to a chair at the dining table. "Varies from alpha to alpha. Some don't care and do nothing, others take that very seriously and take an eye for an eye approach."

"Yeah, I like that last one," Jane said, shifting over to her purse and pulling out the gun she'd used to shoot Harley. "You do anything to that woman and I'll end you, little man," Jane threatened.

Little man? Oh, fuck!

I didn't think Jane knew just how much of an insult that was to a shifter, especially Tank. I could see it in his eyes, how much he wanted to see if Jane would do it. He was debating killing Petra just for fun to see if Jane had the balls to shoot him. But she'd shot Harley, so... Tank slowly set Petra back on his lap and released her. The poor woman gasped and coughed.

"Can't stop me from fucking her," Tank growled and smashed his mouth over Petra's even before she'd regained her breath. He tore away her top with one swipe, grabbing her breast, right there in front of every-one. Jane gaped, horrified. The trouble was, this was stan-dard behavior for Tank.

"Can he do that?" Jane asked.

"He can if Petra's willing," I whispered. Then, as Jane drew breath for her next question, I stopped her. "Don't," I said, keeping my voice low.

Jane glared up at me.

I pulled her aside and whispered, "You were going to ask Petra if she was willing, weren't you? Well, think about that. You think she'd go against a man like Tank? She'd probably say 'yes,' just to appease him, then you gain nothing. And if she dared to say 'no,' that would only lead to more pain from Tank sometime when you're not looking. I know it's disgusting... I know *he's* disgusting... but we need to wait, hard as that is. We'll find a time to get her away from him. You just won a battle. Take the win and regroup for the next battle, there are going to be lots."

Jane was furious. "I won't let him hurt her anymore!" she hissed.

"First, you have to get her away from him. He's made her his mate and she ain't gonna say otherwise while he's in earshot. Wait," I urged her.

I could see how much that burned her. It burned me too. I knew firsthand how cruel and brutal my father was. He'd beaten me half-to-death regularly when I was a kid, telling me it would make me strong. And I'd gotten strong, sure enough, but despite him, not because of him. I hated that man, hated this life, and I hoped Jane would survive long enough to change things.

"What next then?" Jane whispered. "I need to do something or I just might shoot that man!"

"Get everyone organized and settled. Tell them where they'll be staying. Start there," I suggested. She nodded. "And when the time comes, I'll handle my father while you get Petra away."

She nodded again, face hard. I could see now that she was finally starting to understand what it was going to mean to rule this crew. And she didn't like it one bit.

"Tyson, let's get these folks settled!" she called out.

It was a lengthy process, but we eventually got everyone situated.

Tank and Sonny would stay in the living room. There were two couches they could sleep on. Jane had tried to get Petra away from Tank, to stay with the other women — who had been given the large basement rec room — but that hadn't worked. The remaining men, four in all, took the guest room, which was also in the basement. Brick had set up a tent in the back yard. Bronn, Tyson, and I would stay in Jane's room, on the floor, of course. Though, only one of us would ever be in there at a time. During the night, one would stay in with her, another would guard her door, and the third would patrol around, keeping the peace. That meant we'd need to take shifts sleeping. Though, as shifters, we were also okay going without sleep for a while if needed.

The pack didn't have a lot of possessions, only what we could store on our bikes. There were a couple bike trailers in which we stored our group equipment, tents and such, since we'd been living in nature for years now. With so little, we unloaded quickly.

Then we began work on the next challenge: lunch for twenty.

Bronn and I assembled a meal which used up most of what Jane had in her fridge and cupboards.

"Your pack is going to ruin me financially! I can't afford to feed this many people for a week! Doesn't your pack have any funds of its own?" Jane complained to Tyson, Bronn, and I after lunch. We'd retreated to her bedroom. She sat on the edge of the bed, while the three of us stood nearby.

Tyson answered. "We do, yes, but no one knows how much Harley had stashed away. He gave it out sparingly. He probably had a horde somewhere, but only Brick would know where it is, and he isn't going to tell you." Tyson sighed. "I'm sorry Jane, but finding the money to take care of us is going to fall to you as proof you can take care of the pack."

Jane seemed to deflate. She leaned forward, elbows on knees, and ran her hands through that gorgeous soft hair of hers. "Fuck," she whispered. "I have savings, but..."

An idea crept into my head. "Jane," I whispered.

She looked up at me with weary frustration in those large brown eyes.

"Everything the pack has is yours," I said.

"Yeah, but if Brick won't give me the money, then it doesn't matter if it's technically mine or not!"

"I'm not talking about money."

She looked at me confused.

I talked it out, glancing at Tyson and Bronn as I went, wondering if they'd considered this at all. "Look, you don't plan on dying next week, and I'm assuming you don't plan on buying a bike and riding either, you're staying here and probably not selling your house, right?"

She nodded. "Yeah, so?"

"So... if we're not going to be a roving pack anymore... why do we need *our* bikes?"

Bronn gasped.

Tyson's eyes went wide, before he blinked and cocked his head. "You're right. But man, that would piss people off."

"Mostly the old betas," Bronn clarified.

I smiled. "Exactly, and we don't have to sell all the bikes, probably just a few to pay for a week's worth of supplies. Whose bikes do you think we'd start with?" I grinned.

Bronn grinned, catching on.

"Oh man, you're cruel. I love it," Tyson said.

"We sell the old beta's bikes?" Jane said with a vicious little smile of her own.

"Exactly," I said. "Unless Brick wants to tell us where the money is, then we may not have to."

"You're so big, sometimes I forget you have brains," Bronn said.

"Yeah, well... I don't use them a lot, so they're fresh and ready to go when I need them," I joked. Everyone laughed, including Jane. Seeing the smile on her face warmed my heart and made it pound all the faster.

"It's a plan," Jane said. "Let's do it!"

JANE

ALL FOUR OF US WENT TO CONFRONT BRICK. I COULDN'T deny how amazing it felt to have these three strapping men towering around me. Yesterday, if these three had been this close, I'd have been terrified, but a lot had changed in a very short time.

And as much as I'd only known them for a few hours, I was quickly becoming accustomed to them. I didn't know what it meant to be fated, but I certainly felt something for Tyson. Somehow, my soul *knew* the man.

Something deep in my gut told me everything I needed to know about him: I could trust him, he'd always protect me, and he was a sexy beast of a man. Just thinking of him made my heart beat quicker.

When I looked at him, my eyes may have seen a gruff and hard exterior, but I knew he was more than just his brooding bad boy persona. I'd never wanted the bad boys in my younger years. I knew they wouldn't treat me well, but that didn't stop me from drooling over their hard, edgy looks.

And Tyson had all of that going on: tall and broad, with dark hair framing a tanned face and dark, intense, blue eyes. Heat shivered through me just thinking about him. He had all that, and he'd treat me right. Now *that* was the perfect bad boy.

I found it ever-so-ironic that I'd married a man who I'd thought was a good guy and he'd turned out to be a jerk in disguise. Now, I had a man who looked to be one hundred percent bad, but I knew he had a good heart.

And then there were the other two men with me.

Bronn was simply beautiful: rich black skin, a smooth-shaved head and face, with dark eyes, and even though he was the shortest of the three, he was built thick and stocky with heavy shoulders and arms rolling with muscle. He had this way of looking at me, like he wanted to eat me, but in the best way, like I was the sweetest and most tempting dessert.

Behind that look though, deep in his near-to-black eyes, was a pain so deep it made me want to just hold him close and tell him everything would be all right. Then, there'd been our kiss, which somehow had turned into me mock biting his neck. I'd never been more turned on in my entire life and I'd felt that raw desire reciprocated from him. I didn't have some special bond with him, but I knew I could trust him, implicitly, that he was there for me, no matter what.

And last, but so very far from least, there was cheerful, hulking Colt. The giant man was half a head taller than Tyson but built just as stocky as Bronn, which made him absolutely huge. His arms were the size of my — not skinny — thighs.

Yet despite his size, he seemed like a teddy bear, all welcoming warmth. And as Bronn had recently pointed out, there was a brain in his head. A head covered in thick blond locks with steady amber-brown eyes and a square jaw, chiseled from stone. And when those amber eyes looked at me, his mouth would quirk in just a hint of a smile, as if I was a best friend — someone he'd known forever — that he was starting to think could be more. It left me feeling comfortably warm and thrilled all at once.

Just as we stepped out the back door, my phone rang. I stopped and the guys stopped with me.

Pulling out my cell, I looked at the screen. It was Melody Khan. The Khan's were my neighbors, an older couple, who had started this little cul-de-sac community far from the chaos of the city. They took a strong interest in everything that happened on the street and there was no way they'd missed the eighteen bikes parked on my lawn. This should be... interesting.

I accepted the call and put the phone to my ear. "Hello Mrs. Khan," I said trying to sound cheery. Though I could hear the exhaustion setting into my voice.

"Janey, are you okay?" Her concerned voice came over the line. "We... ah... we heard a gun and... and... are you okay?"

I sighed. So, they knew. I wondered how many of our little community had seen me shoot Harley. Or at least seen me with a gun in my hand and a dead man at my feet after they heard the shots and rushed to their windows. The fact that the cops weren't swarming our otherwise quiet cul-de-sac spoke volumes.

Whatever they'd thought of me, they had all accepted that a dead biker wasn't worth getting me in trouble over.

"Yes, Mrs. Khan, I'm okay. I did what I had to, to protect my family and now... I'm doing my best to ah... reform these folks."

"Oh... my..." *Yeah, exactly.* "Well, if there is anything you need, just let me know." Her tone suggested she didn't want to get involved in any of this though, and I couldn't blame her.

"Thanks, Mrs. Khan, I will." Actually, there was one thing she could very easily help with. Melody Khan was a bit of a gossip and I might as well start this rumor mill out the way *I* wanted it to go. "Now that I think of it, Melody, there is something you can do. These folks are going to be staying with me for a few days at least. I'll make sure they don't bother the neighbors too much, but can you let everyone know I'm safe and have things handled for now?"

"Yes, of course." She sounded very happy to be tasked with that.

"Thanks again, Mrs. Khan. I've got to go now, bye."

"Bye."

I hung up and sighed. I had a feeling there would be many more awkward calls or interactions like that in my future. Right now though, I had another awkward and potentially dangerous interaction to focus on.

Two bikes had been rolled back here, along with one trailer. A good-sized tent had been set up and the trailer was under the large canopy at the front. Tarps covered the two bikes.

"Bet he's already claimed Harley's hog," Colt whispered to Bronn.

"No bet." He pointed to one of the tarped bikes. "I'd recognize the shape of Harley's Road King anywhere."

Colt laughed. "Does anything escape you?"

"No." Bronn had this way of speaking, efficient, concise, never more than he needed to say. He seemed so very guarded, even around Tyson and Colt, who were supposed to be his friends.

There was far more to these men than I knew, but I didn't have time to find out now.

"Brick!" Tyson called, standing outside the tent.

It took a long moment for Brick to come out, and when he did, I looked away, because he was buck naked. "What ya want, boy?" Brick growled. Then he laughed. "Looks like our new alpha can't even look me in the... eye."

Tyson confronted his father about the money while Bronn stepped in front of me, shielding my view of the man and whispered. "Shifters have little modesty. We have to strip to change and we all live close, so being naked and seeing others naked doesn't bother us. You need to face Brick down or he'll never submit to you. Just... look him in the eye for now. Can you do that?"

I nodded, drawing myself up as Bronn stepped aside.

Tyson had just finished outlining our deal: hand over the money or we sell your bike.

Brick was livid. I managed to keep my eyes level with his, ignoring everything else. But his attention wasn't on me. "I know this isn't the little bitch's idea. So which one of you dared to think of selling our livelihoods? Our bikes are everything! They're who we are!"

"Not if we're staying here, they aren't," Tyson said, facing down his father.

Looking at the two of them... I could see the resemblance now, but it was faint. Tyson was a bit taller, and Brick was stockier and heavier, a little more run to fat than his son. The older man's hair was long and shaggy like his son, but mostly grey now. The real resemblance was in the eyes. They shared the same eye color as well as the ridge of the brow above. Their noses might have been the same, but both had been broken a few too many times. Tyson's was still mostly straight, but Brick's was a mess of lumps. And certainly, their aggressive auras were a match for each other.

"And we won't *have* to sell them if you hand over Harley's horde," Tyson said. "So really, this is your choice."

The two of them stared each other down for a long moment, all barely restrained male bravado. Then Brick finally backed down with a laugh. "Fine, but you ain't gonna like it!" He backed off and went to the tarped bikes.

We followed.

Lifting the tarp on the one Bronn had identified as Harley's bike, Brick opened one of the side boxes and reached inside, digging around a bit. Tyson pushed him aside and removed everything from inside the box, dumping it on the lawn.

Brick picked up a stack of bills, bundled with a binder clip. He tossed it to Tyson. "That should be roughly five thousand. That's it. That's all Harley had, his entire horde." Brick laughed again. When I looked over at him to see if I could discern whether he was telling the truth, he reached down and cupped his balls.

"If you want anything more than that, alpha, I'll give you everything I've got," he said mocking, suggestive.

"You have nothing I want," I replied and turned away.

We made our way back into the house.

"He's lying, there's more... somewhere," Bronn whispered.

"Yeah, I figured," Tyson said. "But he's probably hidden that away himself. This'll do for now." Tyson handed me the stack of cash, which looked to be a mix of hundreds, fifties, and twenties. "How long will that last?"

I did some quick math in my head. "If it *is* five thousand, that should last the week easily, maybe two, no more." By my estimate it was going to cost roughly four hundred dollars a day to take care of this brood. That was a generous estimate, but something told me these rough folks would add some extra costs that I hadn't yet accounted for. "Which one of you wants to do the shopping? You know what this group eats better than I do."

"I'll go," Bronn said quickly.

I handed over the cash. "Take my car, you'll need the space. The keys are in my purse." I didn't know how or why I fully trusted the man, but I did.

Thinking of my keys and my car reminded me that I wouldn't be going anywhere any time soon. I needed to let my job know I'd be out of commission for a while.

I pulled out my phone again and sent a text to my boss. I told him I was sick, had a high fever and had only just gotten out of bed now. I didn't know how long

I'd be gone. I'd email more details on any open accounts I had.

Hopefully that would keep him off my ass for a while. It was Thursday and I'd be able to get through to the weekend no problem, but next week might be another issue. Though, I could say that my kids got what I'd had and I had to stay home and take care of them. I didn't like the lie, but I had a lot more at stake than my job right now.

Like... my life.

I'd just sent the text when I heard the toilet flush in the bathroom, which was just off the back hall, but toward the front of the house. Tank came out a moment later, which I suspected wasn't long enough for him to have washed his hands, especially since his cock was out and in his hand. His gaze slid over me and he grinned as he made his way back to the living room. I had no clue what he was going to do, but I had a feeling it would be something to test me.

"Petra, bitch, pussy now!"

I immediately glanced at the woman on the couch holding what was left of her shirt around her.

Pleading eyes caught mine for just a moment before she turned to Tank and said, "Yes master," then rose and quickly stripped out of her clothes, it wasn't hard with her shirt already torn and only a mini skirt otherwise. I could see the swell of her stomach. She was probably five or six months along into her pregnancy.

I swore internally, realizing I'd missed my chance to get her away from him.

Tank reached her, turned her around, and bent her

over the couch, taking her right there, no foreplay or preamble. My vagina hurt in sympathetic pain at the thought of a man that big forcing his way into me while I was bone dry down there.

But then again, pain seemed to be Tank's thing. He wasn't kind or gentle at all, one hand grabbed a fistful of Petra's long, dark hair and yanked it, forcing her head back at an awkward angle. She let out a gasp and yelp, which seemed to only arouse him more. And the worst of it all was, he wasn't really paying any attention to Petra. His eyes were on me, watching me, with a grin.

"Do you like to watch, alpha? Wanna see me dump my cum in this bitch? Maybe you'd rather it was you?" Tank leered at me.

I clenched my jaw. I wanted to stare him down, but after what he'd said, that would give him the win. He wanted me to watch. I shook my head and stalked back to my room, knowing I'd just lost another battle. Tank's laughter followed me down the back hall. Tyson and Colt came with me, but Colt stayed outside, guarding the door.

"I'll keep an eye out," he said, as Tyson closed the door.

Inside my bedroom I stormed around. I needed to hit something. "I could have taken her away from him!" I hissed. "I was distracted with dealing with Brick and... ugh!"

Tyson plucked one of the pillows from my bed and came to me. "Hit me," he said stoically, holding the pillow in front of him.

"I'm not going to hit you, I—"

"Hit me," he said again, his tone insistent. I stopped my angry-nervous shifting and looked at him. "Hit me. Then, when your head is clear, we can make some plans."

He was right, I wasn't thinking straight. I couldn't think at all. My mind was crowded with dollar signs, and naked people, and brutes taking advantage of others. I screamed and punched the pillow.

"Harder," Tyson said, not at all fazed by my hit.

I hit again. And it wasn't like I didn't know how to throw a punch. After my ex, Oliver, had left, I'd wanted to make sure I could protect myself and had taken a self-defense course. I knew the basics: how to make a fist and throw a punch, kick 'em in the nuts, a few locks and holds and such.

I pummeled that pillow with both fists for longer than I thought I could, sweaty and bedraggled by the end. I'd even thrown off my suit jacket, continuing with the onslaught. And when I was done, weak and weary, I just wept, falling into Tyson, who held me against him, strong arms enfolding me, holding me close, holding me up, that battered pillow pressed between us.

When my tears dried, he asked, "Better?"

I nodded against his solid chest.

"Time to plan?" he asked.

I nodded again and pulled away from him. That poor pillow was toast now; I'd burst it open and the stuffing was coming out. I couldn't afford to do that too many more times.

I flopped down, sitting on the bed. "Just how... how do I do this?" I asked, feeling defeated. It hadn't even been a full day and I was already at my wits' end.

Tyson climbed onto the bed and crawled behind me. His strong hands came to my shoulders and began massaging sore muscles with vigorous efficiency.

"One day at a time," he said softly. "Today is set up and planning. We'll figure out a rough strategy for the rest of the week. Tomorrow will be implementation. Your betas will put the plan into action while you rest."

"Why am I resting?" I asked. "I get the feeling that won't go over well." Wasn't I supposed to be a strong alpha or something?

"You're resting because I'll have turned you, and you won't be feeling yourself."

"Oh," I said, a shiver running through me. I swallowed a lump in my throat. "Will it hurt?"

"Yes. I won't lie." Yet his voice was soft and low, soothing. "To be sure, I'll need to cut you deep enough for a good bit of blood. I'll do the same to myself and make sure our blood mixes. We can fix you up after that, but that wound is still going to hurt... and you'll start to feel disoriented and dizzy. It will get worse as the day goes on, until the moon rises tomorrow. Then you'll shift. The first time is always painful. Your body is remaking itself. It's like all your bones break at once and all your joints are pulled out."

"I could have done with just a little lying there," I said, sounding meek. The whole thing sounded utterly horrible. "It gets better, though?"

"Yeah. There's always a little pain when you shift, but after a while it's more like a stubbed toe, annoying for a moment, then gone."

"Oh..." I released a heavy breath. "Good."

"But tomorrow will probably be the worst pain of your life. You can ask my mom what the pain was like compared to childbirth. Then you'll be a wolf and you'll want to hunt. You'll be ravenous. We can let you loose out in the woods. That would be best, so you can really get a sense for the hunt or, if you like, we can stock up on steaks and just feed you here. The pack would probably think you a weak alpha, though. We only do that when we're trapped somewhere without nature. When we have to."

"I think staying in will be better, no matter what it looks like to the pack. I'm more worried about what it will look like to my neighbors if you're carrying me off into the woods while I look like I'm dying. They didn't call the cops on me for killing Harley, but I think more than a few would call them if they saw that."

He grunted. "Hmmm, yeah, you're probably right." He sighed. "We'll make it work."

"Okay, so... rest, shift, eat. Then what?" Did I want to know?

"Saturday you'll be tired again, but you'll recover quicker, since you'll be a wolf. We betas will still be implementing your plan. Sunday you'll come out as a full wolf and show dominance. Nothing big, but get your scent on everything you can, claim your house, your pack, everything. I'll also start teaching you about your forms and how to fight. After that we'll have three days to get you into fighting shape for the challenge."

"It doesn't sound like a long time," I said. "Realistically, do you think I can do it?"

He was silent for too long, his hesitation speaking louder than words. "You have to."

And that's when I knew, whatever I expected the next week to be like, it was going to be a hundred times worse. I was going to have to push myself harder than I ever had if I wanted to survive.

JANE

I took a bit of time to regain my composure. My mascara was a mess from my crying fit earlier, so, since I wasn't going to work and I didn't care what I looked like, I removed all my make-up.

Tyson stood behind me while I sat at my vanity. He smiled at my bare features and kissed the top of my head softly. "You're beautiful, just as you are," he whispered.

That was a bit much from a man I'd only met that morning, and yet it was more than my husband had ever said to me. I blushed. Tyson was a fit, handsome man in his prime. I was an aging mother with laugh lines and stretch marks. I had no clue how we were going to make this work.

"You're only saying that because you're fated for me," I said, deflecting the compliment.

He actually took a moment to consider this. "Perhaps," he said in all seriousness. "I'm not sure I can recall what you looked like before. I... don't think I'd ever looked at you for any length of time. There was no point to it. You were human, I wasn't. Even if you'd been the most gorgeous woman in the world, we couldn't have been together. It may be that the fated bond has changed how I see you. Does that matter?"

Did it?

I suppose... it didn't. He saw me as beautiful now and that's all that really mattered.

"What is this fated bond?" I'd been meaning to ask since that morning.

"You'd have to ask my mom," Tyson said with a grimace. "In truth, I only found out about it just before you did. I know very little, other than I feel compelled to be with you, close to you, to protect you and support you and—"

"Fuck me?" I supplied, feeling more heat rise to my cheeks. In the mirror, I watched a visceral shudder roll through his body, and his hands came up to capture the tops of my arms in a possessive grip.

"Yes," he breathed. "The urge to mate with you is... very strong."

I had a *very strong* urge to *mate* with him as well.

Heat flooded me, then seemed to sink and pool in my core. God, I hadn't been this aroused since... well, since my kiss with Bronn that morning.

But before that, it had been a very, *very* long time. My ex had loved having sex... up until I'd had Izzy. After that, it had been like pulling teeth to get him to be close. I'd thought another kid would help our relationship. I'd been wrong. He'd walked out, leaving me for some girl from his gym — who was half my age — when Milo had been three.

"But I can't," Tyson said, breaking the moment. I could see the iron bands of restraint holding him back, his body shaking with the effort. "You're not a wolf yet."

"And when I am?" I asked, my curiosity fueled by this raging storm of wet heat pulsing through me.

"You'll need to be training to fight, not mating with me. Once Brick is out of the picture, then..." He trailed off.

For some reason, that seemed like *way* too long. Yesterday, I would have thought sleeping with a guy I'd only known for a week was *way* too soon. But that had been before magical fated mating bonds had been a thing, so...

"I understand," I said. I certainly wasn't going to force him. But it was kind of nice to have this brooding, sexy, kind-hearted man literally shaking with desire for me.

The moment passed and he stepped back as I rose.

"Okay, let's get things started," I said.

Tyson nodded, opening the door to my room to speak to Colt, who gathered my kids from their rooms and brought them to my bedroom. Colt stayed outside as I got my kids settled so we could talk.

The three of us sat cross-legged on my bed while Tyson stood, leaning against the wall by the door. Milo was smiling and bright-eyed, practically bouncing, but poor Isabella looked a wreck, trembling, eyes red-rimmed from crying.

I had no clue how the three of us were going to get through this, but that was one of the reasons I'd called them in. As much as I wanted them to be kids forever, at sixteen and thirteen, they were old enough to act like adults if the situation called for it. And I agreed with Tyson who'd suggested we bring them in on our plans to make sure the whole family was together on this. I was touched that he'd thought of them.

Yet now that they were here, I had no clue how to even begin this discussion. I looked over at Tyson, all calm, easy strength, confident. Nothing like me.

"Just talk," he said. "They're old enough to understand all of this."

I nodded and turned back to my kids.

"I think you both have a good idea what's going on, but just in case, I'm going to clarify a few things." I looked from one to the other and they nodded. "First, I... I..." God, it was hard to say. My throat closed up and I got all cold and hot at the same time. "I killed a man."

There, I'd said it.

After that, things came out in a rush. "I did it to protect you both. I didn't have a choice. It was my life or his and if he won, he was going to claim you both, take you away, and I couldn't allow that. I hope you can understand though I don't expect you to wave it off. I certainly can't. It was horrid and... the worse thing I've ever done in my life and I'll have to live with that. I'm sorry if that traumatized you."

"You're such a badass mom!" Milo said, excited.

I really didn't understand teen boys.

Then he calmed a little. "But I know it's bad." He swallowed heavily. "I... I'm sorry I caused all this trouble."

I nodded. We'd come back to that in a moment.

I looked at Izzy, tears welling in her eyes. She tried to speak a few times before, finally, voice strained and tears on her cheek, she squeaked, "You were protecting us. I know. It was—"

She shook, unable to speak. I slid over the bed to her and gathered her up in my arms. She melted into me, crying fully. I smoothed her hair and held her, like Tyson had done for me not that long ago.

It had been a while since Izzy had let me hold her like this. She'd been going through a phase, exerting her independence and testing boundaries, and we'd fought more than we'd talked recently. So, it was nice to just hold her again, like I had when she'd been younger.

When she could speak again, she finished her previous sentence. "It was awful, but then... seeing that monster in our living room. That..." she said, her shaking returning, and I held her closer. I understood now. It wasn't any one event from today that had cracked her usually tough exterior, but all of it. I'd seen how horrified she'd been when Tyson had shifted.

"You know he's not a monster now, right?" I asked softly. "Tyson is helping me. He's on our side."

She nodded against my chest. I wasn't sure if she really believed me. "But the others... they're so loud and..." She shivered.

I think I understood. She'd been hiding in her room all morning. A room which shared a wall with the living room. She'd probably heard all of Brick and Tank's crass and horrid remarks.

"I know," I whispered. "That's why we're talking now, to make sure you're safe and to make sure we have a plan for what to do about all of this."

She nodded against my chest again.

Milo brightened. "Does that mean I get to be a wolf?"

"No!" Tyson and I said in unison.

But that led to the next most important part. "But I *will* have to become one, so I can defend myself. In a week anyone will be able to challenge me for leadership of the pack, and if I die, you both belong to them. I can't let that happen, and I won't, you understand me? I absolutely will not leave you."

Milo seemed to shrink a little, subdued. "Oh... really? You need to fight?"

"Yes."

"To protect us?" Izzy asked through her tears.

"Yes." And to save my own life.

Izzy cried a little more. I waited for her to get it all out. It took a while. Then she sat up on her own, sniffling, eyes red.

"Are you okay to make some plans?" I asked.

She nodded, jaw tight, a hint of her usual mettle hardening her brown eyes. Good, she'd need it.

She wiped her tears on her sleeves. "What do we do?" she asked.

That was an excellent question. I turned to Tyson. "I'm open to suggestions. You know the pack better than I do."

He nodded. "First thing is to make sure these pups are protected." That was an excellent place to start.

"You can call them kids," I said. Pups just reminded all of us he was a werewolf, which I didn't think was helping.

Tyson nodded looking at Milo. "Hey, kid."

That hadn't been what I'd meant. "Please call him Milo," I asked.

Tyson seemed to stiffen a little. I got the feeling it wasn't because he didn't want to, but more... he seemed a bit afraid of that level of intimacy.

"Milo." He tested the word.

"Yeah? I mean... yes, sir?" Milo said.

I tried not to laugh at that. Milo had never been that deferential to anyone. I was a bit surprised.

"How'd you like a dog?"

"Sir?" Milo asked.

I was curious where Tyson was going with this. I raised my brow in question at the tall, dark man. He smiled back.

"My brother, Brutus," Tyson said to both me and Milo. "He's a good man, and I know he's not close with our father." Tyson addressed this next bit to me. "You remember how Brick was so adamant about bikes being our lives? Well, that's just one part of it, the other part is shifting, being a wolf. Brutus hates the bikes. He'd rather be a wolf all the time. I say... let's let him. I'm certain he'd be grateful for it. The only condition... he needs to stay by Milo's side and protect him. I'm fairly certain Brutus will agree to that."

I wasn't sure how I felt about a wolf going everywhere Milo did, but I did like my boy having a constant minder and protector. I trusted Tyson — that seemed to come with being fated — so I'd let him do this.

I nodded.

Milo gave a whoop. "Yeah! Nice! I get a wolf!"

That was taken care of.

Tyson squirmed for a moment then said, "Izzy?"

Again, it seemed like he felt awkward being so informal with my kids.

She looked at him and I caught something in her gaze. She'd been through a lot today, but she was still a hormonal teenager. There was a strange mix of fear and lust in that look, neither of which was surprising. Tyson was a very handsome man, if you liked the dark and dangerous type. As for the fear, that made sense too. Apparently, she couldn't quite separate him from the monster she'd seen earlier, not yet at least.

"Yes?" she said through her sniffles.

Tyson looked back and forth between me and my daughter. "I was thinking my sister might tag along with you. She won't be a wolf, just herself, but she's a tough bitch, and—"

"Language, please," I admonished Tyson.

He blinked. "What?" It seemed to take him a long moment to understand. "Oh... ah... you may need to get used to that word. It's common for us to refer to the women of the pack as bitches, the men are simply dogs. There's no real male equivalent of the word. That one may be hard for us to cut out. It's not meant offensively... most of the time."

"Oh."

"So, once she's turned, Mom will be a bitch?" Milo said, a little too excited to be saying that. I spun on him, staring him down, and he quelled himself.

Tyson cleared his throat. "Ah... yeah, she would."

Izzy cracked a smile, just for a moment. I could tell she was going to use the hell out of that now. Great.

I sighed. "Go on," I said to Tyson.

"Ah... yes, well, my sister doesn't take crap from anyone and she can defend herself well. She probably should have been the next alpha instead of me, but my pack — or the old alpha at least — still had some feelings about women being in charge... which we're going to rectify soon." That last bit was tacked onto the end just a little too hastily.

"We'd better," I mumbled. To Izzy, I asked. "Would you be okay with a roommate for a while." To Tyson I asked, "how old is your sister, and which one is she?" I'd met the entire pack today and most were still a jumble in my head.

"Her name is Rita, she's thirty-seven."

Ah... so not really a contemporary for my daughter, but old enough to know how to handle herself, hopefully.

"I guess that's okay," Izzy said with a shrug. My daughter liked her privacy, and I knew this was asking a lot of her. Izzy gave a bit of a harrumph. "This is all just so..." she gave a loud groan.

"I know," I said.

Izzy made an annoyed sound but didn't say anything else.

"I guess that's settled," I said to both Izzy and Tyson. Then, just because I really didn't know how old Tyson was... I pried a little. "So, your *younger* sister will—"

"No, she's older than me, by three years."

Oh...

Oh!

I knew he *looked* young and strong and virile, but...

that meant he was at least ten years younger than I was. Oh, Lord. What was I getting myself into?

"And Bronn and Colt?" I asked, unable to help myself.

Bronn seemed older, perhaps because of his serious and brooding demeanor, while Colt seemed like a young buck, but perhaps he was older than he looked?

"Bronn's thirty. Colt's twenty-eight."

Lord Almighty, that was young indeed. Colt was closer to Izzy's age than mine! I couldn't possibly be with them... and I shouldn't. I already had a fated mate... whatever that was. And one was enough, right?

That didn't stop my mind from fantasizing though. My dirty, betraying, lustful mind conjured images of Bronn and Colt together, naked, pressed against me. Bronn's hard body crushed against my chest, with Colt hard and ready at my back. Their hands and lips roamed and kissed. Their rigid erections dug into my—

I quickly pushed those thoughts away and concentrated on what was important: my kids.

"So, your siblings will look after my kids. Thank you, Tyson."

"I still have to talk to them about it and see if they agree, but I think it'll work."

"And you're both good with this?" I asked my kids.

Milo nodded enthusiastically.

Izzy sighed and grumbled, far from thrilled. "Any idea how long this would be for?"

I had no clue, but luckily Tyson answered. "Once we're past a week, we'll know more. If there isn't anyone left in the pack you need to be afraid of, then you won't need protection."

Izzy groaned "oh great," and seemed to shrink in on herself again.

She wasn't happy, but she'd be safe and that was all I cared about for now. Happiness could come later... once I'd defeated Brick.

If I defeated Brick.

TYSON

THE REST OF THE PLAN FOR THE NEXT COUPLE DAYS WAS sketched out. Tomorrow the kids would go back to school as usual, if only to get them out of the house for a while. Their protectors would stay here, of course. The kids weren't in any danger at school, well, not from the pack anyway. Then I'd turn Jane and she'd rest while Bronn, Colt, and I started talking to the pack.

I'd said I'd try to convince them to come to Jane's side, but Jane had had a much better idea. She wanted to know what the pack members actually wanted. That was an idea that had never even occurred to me.

Choice and the *freedom to choose* was a completely foreign concept to me, and probably for the pack as well. We'd always had an alpha telling us what to do.

But Jane was different. She didn't want to control us. She wanted everyone to have a choice. They could follow her or do as they wished. There would be no repercussions for "abandoning" the pack. That said, pack was pack and I didn't think anyone would want to leave.

Still though, that power to choose was significant. I honestly didn't know how well it would go over, but I'd said I'd find out what people truly wanted and bring that information back to her. Once we knew that, we could plan further.

That meant I'd also have to figure out what *I* wanted. It was startling to realize I'd never really thought about that. I'd always been told how things would be. I'd assumed I'd be a different sort of alpha than Harley when I took over, but since I'd never thought about *how exactly* I'd be different, perhaps I wouldn't have been. It gave me lots to think about.

And, while I asked around tomorrow, Bronn and Colt would run interference with the old betas, making sure they weren't affecting people's decisions. We'd also try to free Petra if we could. If time permitted, I'd go over a bit more of what it meant to be a wolf with Jane as well.

That decided, the kids stayed with Jane for a bit while I went to talk to my brother and sister. I didn't know where Brutus was, but I was fairly certain Rita was in the basement.

When I turned the corner at the bottom of the stairs into the large rec room, I could already see they had done some redecorating. The chairs had all been moved to the sides of the room and our blankets and sleeping kits had been laid out in an orderly fashion on the carpeted floor. There was one long couch, on which Ginny lounged. That had probably been a concession to the mate of the now-dead alpha to keep her from making too much of a stink.

"Rita!" I called out, to get my sister's attention.

She turned and headed toward me. My mom caught my gaze and nodded. The other three females in the room all instantly deferred to me, bowing a little, even Dana Juarez. I highly suspected she was a dominant type, but she'd learned not to question an alpha or beta. This is what Jane didn't understand, the ingrained hierarchy which had been crushed into our beings all our lives. I honestly didn't know what these folks would think of being given a choice of what to do.

"Brother," Rita's tone was clipped and cold, which wasn't uncommon for her. Brick had raised us all to be hard. Even our mom had reinforced that we'd need to be strong and tough. She'd tried to give us any comfort she could, but the message was always clear: comfort is for those rare moments when you're not fighting for your life.

And Rita was one hard woman. She kept her dark hair short, hacked back haphazardly with a knife. Her eyes were a few shades of blue lighter than mine, in a face of hard planes and old scars. Like my mom, she was built firm, square, strong.

"How would you feel about staying with our new alpha's daughter, Izzy? She'll need a protector and someone to show her the ropes of our pack, but she's not a wolf and will need a bit of a softer touch."

Rita raised a single brow, clearly skeptical.

"I know *soft* isn't your thing, but perhaps she can teach you a little while you teach her? If this all works out, we may not need to be on guard all the time anymore. But all that aside, she needs someone to protect her from the old betas and I know you're the toughest bitch we have."

Rita puffed up a little at that compliment, then slowly let out a breath, not responding right away, instead nodding toward the stairs.

We went up, then out the side door of the house. She clearly didn't want anyone else to hear what she had to say.

"You really think this soft human woman will last longer than a week?" she asked. She'd always been forthright, to the point.

She has to, I thought, but that answer wouldn't suffice for Rita. Instead, I asked, "Has mom told you about... what happened to me? Why I supported the new alpha so quickly?"

Rita shook her head.

Good. My mom was smart, shrewd, and careful. She wouldn't speak of me being fated where any wolf could overhear. Our hearing was exceptional after all.

"I'm fated for her, Rita," I said, voice hushed. "And in case you don't know what that means — because I didn't — the short version is, if she dies, I'll probably go insane. So, do I think she can win? No, probably not, not yet anyway. Does she *have to* win? Yes."

Rita let out a low whistle. "Fuck."

She turned away, hand combing through her short hair as she took this in. After several deep breaths and long sighs, she turned back to me.

"I'm no good with kids," she said. "I mean, there were never any good candidates for me to mate in our pack, but even if there had been, I don't know if I would have mated with anyone. I don't want that sort of attachment. I've never wanted kids, and—"

"Izzy is sixteen. She's young yes, but old enough to know what's going on. She'll need to grow up fast and learn how to be a tough young woman. You were able to best father one time in five at her age. Teach her that. Teach her how to survive and be a wolf."

"But she's not a wolf!" Rita hissed. "Unless you want me to turn her?"

"No," I said adamantly.

"Then what can I do? She's soft and weak. There isn't anything I can teach her that will help her survive if Tank or Brick go after her."

I knew that.

I sighed. "Then... just keep an eye on her for a week. After that, hopefully this will all be resolved one way or another."

"And if your woman loses and you go mad, and this kid is pulled into the pack, what then?"

I didn't want to think about that, but Rita was right, we needed to plan for everything.

"Then..." I'd have to talk to Jane to confirm anything, but... "Do whatever you'd do if she were your sister."

Rita huffed out a breath, then slowly drew another one. "You know that would probably kill me." I could see it in her eyes, the prospect of defying our father and the calculation of her chances of surviving.

"You're tough," was all I said.

She tilted her head, running her tongue around her teeth inside her mouth. Then she huffed a sigh. "Fine, I'll do this for you." She quickly caught my eye. "For *you*, brother, not the new alpha. I still don't know how I feel about her. The fact that she's somehow fated to you makes me very wary of her. And I still don't think she'll survive the week."

"Thank you, Rita. Go get your things. You'll be staying in Izzy's room. Now, I need to talk to Brutus."

"I'll find him and send him along," she said, then left.

My brother found me a few minutes later. He looked bored. I took after our mom, tall and lean. He took after our father, shorter and stocky. His unkempt sandy-brown hair was longer than mine, past his shoulders, grey-blue eyes blinking sleepily. Since he much preferred being a wolf, he'd never much cared for his human appearance. His teeth were jagged, his beard patchy and half-grown in.

"Bro," he said with a sniff, and I got the distinct impression Rita had roused him from a nap.

"How would you like to be a wolf full time?" I asked.

That sparked some life into his steely eyes. He smiled, showing all his uneven teeth. Some might think he looked scary, but I knew better. He was a hard man, yes, but really, he just wanted to be a wolf and forget the cares of this human world. "Hell yeah, I would!"

"The only catch is... you have to protect our new alpha's son, Milo, at all costs, even from our father. Can you do that?"

Brutus shrugged. "Dad's old." And apparently that was all he had to say about that. "So I get to be a wolf all the time. I just need to protect the boy? Sounds easy enough. Done!" And he stripped and shifted, right there in the driveway.

I sighed, hoping none of the neighbors had seen that. Then I collected his things and opened the side door for him, escorting him to Jane's room. Rita came along a few moments later.

We sorted everything out and got the kids to their rooms. Rita was already dictating rules to Izzy. Somehow, I didn't think that was going to go over well. Milo was scratching Brutus behind an ear. Brutus growled, but only for a moment before tilting his head into the scratch and huffing his contentment. That pairing just might work.

"What now?" Jane asked as I heard her car pulling into her lane.

"Bronn's back with food," I said. A trace of disappointment shifted across her features.

She'd wanted time alone with me. I knew because I wanted the same thing.

Although a part of me was worried. She'd changed into more comfortable clothes before her talk with her kids, and even just watching her now, with no make-up, hair mussed up, and in her sweats, I wanted her.

I wanted to tear off her clothes, turn her over, sniff her sweet pussy, then ram my rock-hard cock into that pussy and drive her mad with pleasure. And I was fairly certain a part of her wanted the same thing. I smelled it on her, the faint whiff of arousal under the constant scent of grass and sun, still covered a little by her lavender perfume. My need to mate her, make her mine, had been growing all day, a pull which was harder and harder to resist.

"I guess we should help him, and for a crew this big

we might as well start supper now, it's going to take a bit of prep." She rose and glided over to me. I was blocking the doorway and didn't move.

She put a hand on my chest, not with any strength, not trying to move me, but needing that contact as much as I did. Her hand slid over my shirt, under my cut, feeling the hills of my muscles. Even just this, her palm over my shirt, made my heart thunder, my body swell with heat.

That hand slid up to my neck, below my ear, as she took another half step, and the fabric of her sweatshirt, pulled taut over her full bust, brushed against me.

She gasped, her arousal spiking. Mine immediately followed suit once I smelled sex on her. I couldn't help it and I pushed my hips in a little, letting her feel the rigidity of my erection against her belly.

"I..." she whispered, her breath ragged.

Just seeing the flush on her cheeks, the rise and fall of her chest, the dilation of her eyes, made me go mad for just a moment. I grabbed her waist and pivoted with her, pinning her against the wall just inside her room. My hand came to her chin tilting it up as my lips descended to claim her mouth. Her hand on my neck pulled me down, and she opened to me, lips and body, her legs parting just a little.

I pushed one leg in closer, crushing against the heated apex of her thighs, and my tongue dove into her mouth, dominating it, seeking every wet corner.

The soft moan that escaped her resonated in my very soul as I rocked my shaft against her belly. I wanted to be inside her, sheathed in her wet warmth, urging her to untold heights of passion. My cock ached for it, painfully hard.

And she wanted it too, given how her hands slid under my shirt and her fingers dug into my sides to urge me closer. Her leg hitched, her thigh pressing up outside of mine, and my leg, pressed to her core, felt her pussy pulse with growing heat.

My hand on her chin slid down to crush against the fullness of her breast. There was too much fabric between us, but still she gasped into my mouth at my touch. Then I slid my other hand down into the waistband of her sweatpants, feeling the silky fabric of her panties as I sought deeper. I dug my fingers into the softness of her ass, gripping her tight and hearing her whine of aroused approval.

Gods, I was losing it. I shifted my leg back a bit, so I could slide the hand in her pants around to her pussy. I was still over her panties, but when my fingers brushed over the soaked fabric covering her slit, she practically vibrated with desperate need.

This was it. We'd gone too far. We were going to fuck right here, right now. We were both desperately tearing at our clothes when—

Colt cleared his throat a bit too loudly on the other side of the bedroom door. "Ah, Bronn's back?" he said firmly.

His words broke the moment. It took every ounce of restraint I had, but I pulled back from Jane, panting hard. Her chest was rising and falling with equal intensity and for a moment it was all I could see. Then I tore my gaze away to focus on anything but her.

"Ah... yes," Jane said. "Thanks Colt." She reached out again, but this time didn't touch me. Her hand curled into a fist as she whispered, "Later?"

Her whispered question echoed what I'd said to her after our first kiss, when she'd confirmed me as her beta, but she didn't sound entirely certain. I could understand that. She'd only known me a few hours but our fated nature was bringing us together far faster than either of us was ready for.

"Promise," I repeated what she'd said to me earlier.

She nodded and we both straightened ourselves up then made our way out to help Bronn with the large load of groceries.

DINNER WAS BOTH RAUCOUS AND QUIET. JUST THE NOISE OF everyone eating was nearly overwhelming. We devoured a stack of steaks, a small mountain of baked potatoes and some corn, but no one spoke.

Afterward, Kira organized the clean-up. Her eyes directed me to take care of my alpha and I did... but after what had happened between us when Bronn got back, I was reconsidering my plans for the evening.

We retreated to her room. This time Bronn stood guard outside while Colt helped keep the peace otherwise. I closed the door and leaned against it. Jane quickly made her way to the far side of the room, behind the bed. If she felt like I did with every nerve-ending on fire, that might explain why she'd gone so far away, and why she began pacing.

"That supper must have cost a fortune," she said. The words were meaningless, just filler.

"I should go," I said. "Someone else can watch you tonight."

That got an instant reaction. She practically ran to me but stopped before we touched again. "No, Tyson, I can't..."

I heard the unsaid words, *I can't be without you.*

My heart said the same thing, and I pulled my hands behind me, tightly grasping one arm to keep myself restrained. If I didn't stay in control, I'd smooth her hair or cup her cheek or stroke an arm or hip or...

"If I stay," I said, voice husky with need. "I'll fuck you. Do you want that?"

It was the truth. I wouldn't be able to resist her all night. During the day, there were tasks to occupy me, things to do, but just lying here, in the same room as her, I wouldn't be able to hold myself back.

Her breath caught. She probably wasn't used to men proclaiming such things so blatantly.

She wet her lips, pink tongue darting out, then curling back in. I could see her struggle. Those large brown eyes looked up to mine, then darted away, over and over. She wanted me to stay, or some part of her did. But another part was fighting it, just as I fought my own pull.

I wanted her, but fought it, because Jane deserved more than just fucking. She deserved something I didn't yet know how to give... love.

She swallowed hard then nodded. "Then perhaps you should go and have someone else watch me." She trembled through a sigh and looked over at her bedside clock. "It's early, but I don't know what else I'm going to do this evening. I'll slip out to the bathroom and start getting ready for bed. When I come back... someone else can be here."

I hated that idea. I wanted to be the one with her, near her, but I also knew this would be best... for now.

"Yeah," I said with a nod and stepped aside so she could leave.

Once the door had closed behind her the tension left me. Well, most of the tension. My cock was still rock hard. I'd need to tend to that myself later.

I stepped out into the hall. "Bronn, you stay with her tonight. I... need some time to think. I'll have Colt keep an eye on the hall here." Then I left to find Colt.

As I passed the bathroom, my overly keen ears heard stifled, ragged breaths and wet rubbing, which I was fairly certain was Jane masturbating.

I almost came at that realization, my cock painfully full and hard. I grunted and quickly moved on. As much as I'd go insane if anything happened to Jane... waiting for her just might drive me mad first.

JANE

Leaning back on the toilet, eyes closed, running my fingers around my clit while imagining they were Tyson's, I shuddered through a somewhat satisfactory orgasm and sighed. I'd desperately needed a release since that steamy moment with him that afternoon, and I'd been in a suspended state of anticipatory hunger — and not for food — ever since.

As a woman in my mid-forties, I sometimes needed the help of lube if I wanted to stimulate myself, but not this time. My panties had been soaked through since Tyson and I had nearly given in to our desires, hours ago. I couldn't stop thinking about him.

Was this what it meant to be fated? It was the most exquisite torture. I'd never felt anything like this for any man... ever. Even my ex-husband had never gotten me this wet. I'd hardly been able to think since Tyson had pinned me against the wall and kissed me. I hadn't been thinking at all in that moment, only feeling the burn of his presence on my ever-so-sensitive... everything.

Sending him away just now had taken every ounce of willpower I'd possessed.

And I still wasn't sure if it had been the right decision. My head said yes, but my heart and body said something else entirely. My blood boiled for Tyson, and right now, I would have taken any man, just to fill this aching void in my core. Luckily, I'd been taking care of my own urges for ten years now and knew what I needed.

I sighed again, feeling marginally better now that I'd gotten myself off. Perhaps now I could regain a bit of composure and rest tonight. Though, given everything I'd gone through today, I wasn't so sure how easy it would be to sleep. Added to my unexpected arousal were heady doses of fear and adrenaline.

I went through my evening routine, hoping those familiar actions would help calm me. Perhaps it was a good thing I was doing everything a couple hours early, it might just take me that long to get to sleep.

When I returned to my bedroom, Colt was in the hall and Bronn was in my room. He leaned against the door once I'd closed it, his eyes on me, thrilling me in an entirely different way than what I'd felt with Tyson.

This strange fated thing Tyson and I shared gripped me in the gut in a primal way, making me need him whether I wanted it or not. But Bronn was quiet and observant. I didn't think he missed much, and the way he looked at me, like I was delectable but unobtainable — forbidden fruit — made me feel alluring and powerful.

I needed to get changed. The part of me that was utterly exhausted after the day's events briefly considered just sleeping in my sweats, but I really needed a new pair of underwear. I opened my mouth to ask Bronn to turn around so I could change... then stopped myself.

What had he said earlier? *...being naked and seeing others naked doesn't bother us.* If I was going to become a wolf, like them... perhaps I should start living like they did?

I pulled out my sleepwear from my dresser: a comfy cotton sports bra, a matching pair of panties, and some loose yoga pants. Closing the blinds over my windows, I took a deep breath.

This is normal, I told myself. *It's just skin, nothing is more natural and normal than that. You can do this, don't make it awkward.*

I just did it. Stripping efficiently out of my sweats and old underwear.

An odd, strangled sound came from the other side of the room and I paused as I looked over at Bronn. In the gloom of the room, I couldn't see too much, but I could make out his wide eyes, the whites clear against his dark skin, his pupils dilated. I also made out the slight shift in his stance. I knew that movement: men trying to adjust themselves without using their hands. And wow, did he have something to adjust, the bulge in his jeans was massive.

And there I was, naked, staring at him.

Suddenly I felt *very* seen. Heat rushed through me, the awkward, embarrassed kind, as I turned away from Bronn. The trouble was, I'd laid my clothes out on the bed behind me.

I reached back, blind, patting the sheets until I found my panties, they needed to be first. As I slid them on, I found words slipping from my lips before I even knew what I was asking. "I thought you said being naked and seeing others naked doesn't bother you."

He cleared his throat, awkward, a little too loud. "Usually doesn't," he said, voice a little strained still.

Which meant it was me... *just me.*

Somehow, forty-four-year-old me, with my slightly sagging tits and stretch marks, heavy hips and thick thighs was turning him on... where other women didn't. I had no clue what to make of that.

It's because I'm new, I told myself. *He's used to seeing the women around him naked, even if they are younger and prettier. But he hasn't seen me naked before, so... I'm just different and somehow, that's arousing for him.*

Sure, yeah, that made sense. Why else would a man in his prime — Tyson had said he was thirty — look at an older woman like me like that?

I finished my awkward dressing, finding the other clothes and putting them on before turning around again.

Oddly, he still looked uncomfortable, eyes still wide.

Again, words tumbled out before I thought about them. "Do you think I'm pretty?" I asked. Some part of me had to know why he'd reacted like that.

"Yes," he said without any hesitation. "It's also your..." He stopped himself, clearly uncertain what to say. "I... I..." He stammered for a moment. "Ah... we shifters have enhanced senses and..." He swallowed. "You look amazing, dressed or not," he said, finally finding words. "But your scent is... intoxicating."

My scent?

"What do I smell like?" I asked. Though as soon as I did, I regretted it. I probably smelled like sweat and fear and sex. But he answered before I could take back my question.

"Spring," he said quickly. "Like a spring morning, dewy grass and the warm sun on exposed skin."

"Oh." I hadn't expected that at all.

He swallowed hard again. I could see his eyes dilating as he spoke, proof of his stimulation. "And right now, you smell like a summer's rainfall. The sweet scent of sun-warmed grasses after a storm." He was shifting again, clearly uncomfortable.

"What?" I asked. There was something he wasn't saying.

"You're... aroused."

I froze.

Aroused?

All the metaphorical *hot* and *damp* conditions he'd described made a lot more sense: *summer's rainfall... after a storm...*

He sighed heavily. "I've made you uncomfortable." His gaze fell to the floor and he shook his head. "I'm sorry. I'm not used to talking to an alpha, to a woman, to anyone." A sharp pain filled his words.

Suddenly, all the awkwardness I'd felt about being naked and smelling of... whatever, was gone.

"Why?" I asked as I sat on my bed, grabbing a pillow and hugging it to my chest, curling my legs under me.

For a long time, Bronn didn't say anything. He was a study in opposites: sturdy and strong on the outside, but clearly fragile and broken on the inside, forward but awkward, knowledgeable of some things, but ignorant of others.

When he did look up again, the pain written clearly on his features broke my heart. Unlike Tyson and Colt, Bronn's face was more rounded, full lips and cheeks, a strong nose, even the fact that he was shaved bald gave him a softer appearance. But there were scars on his face, physical ones long healed, and now his emotional ones were showing as well.

The mother in me, the part that had spent sixteen years caring and tending and soothing, took over.

"You can tell me," I whispered.

I patted the bed next to me, beckoning him. I felt more comfortable now with the pillow covering me. I wouldn't mind if he was a bit closer.

He came, but more like a whipped puppy than a willing man.

"Yes, alpha," he whispered as he came and sat on the edge of the bed, closer, but still out of reach.

Those words, and how he'd said them, spoke volumes.

"Bronn, I may be your alpha, but you know I'll never hurt you, right?"

Then it occurred to me he had no proof of that. Just that morning he'd seen me shoot his old alpha.

He looked at me with a glimmer of hope in his eyes. "I want to believe that."

I finished for him. "But that's never been what you've known, has it?"

He shook his head. "Alpha's aren't kind. They're brutal, especially to those who aren't wolves."

"You're not—?" I stopped myself. Something Tyson had mentioned earlier that day came back to me. He'd mentioned that some in this pack were werebears and there was one werelion. I didn't even know what instinct I drew on then, but I just *knew*... "You're a lion."

He looked at me, brows drawing together. "How...? Humans usually can't tell."

I shrugged. "Call it woman's intuition? I don't know."

He nodded. "I am, yes. And despite lions being bigger than wolves, there are a lot more of *them*." His voice grew faint. "And they made sure I knew it... often."

I didn't know what to say to that.

"I was taken from my pride when I was sixteen," he whispered. For just a flash of a moment, a smile appeared, then vanished. "I loved my family. Prides are ruled by a collective of females, did you know that?" He looked over and I shook my head. "There is an alpha male, sort of, but he's chosen by the females as their primary protector. Other males may also follow the alpha and, just like with wolves, the culture isn't always pretty. Males challenge each other for dominance and whoever wins, wins. The females only want the best and strongest warriors as their alphas. The alpha is also the one who... gets access to the females. My father was an alpha and my mother was the respected eldest of the pride females. They were both killed when Harley's pack fought ours. Harley claimed me as his prize and loved to remind me I was just a lowly cat as often as he could."

"I'm so sorry, Bronn," I said, feeling the need to reach out to him. I shuffled over a bit so I could put a hand on his shoulder. His leather vest was cold under my fingers and his eyes were wet with unshed tears when he looked at me.

"Your kind now, but I fear..."

He feared what? That I'd stop being kind?

"What?" I asked when he didn't go on.

"That after you're turned, you'll be a wolf and..."

Oh.

"I also fear what you'll have to become to defeat someone like Brick..."

Oh.

I hadn't thought about that. Did becoming a shifter change a person? Obviously yes, there was a physical change, but did their temperament and behavior change as well? Tyson had said this was a curse and he'd implied that those who had it were inherently evil. If that was the case... then would I become evil too? Would I no longer feel the compassion and kindness I felt now?

Yet... despite what he'd said, I didn't think Tyson was evil, nor Bronn or Colt. I didn't know what to believe. Suddenly, I desperately needed to find out.

"Does turning a person usually change them?" I asked, tentative.

Bronn shrugged, his heavy shoulder muscles moving under my hand. "I don't know. I wasn't witness to any turnings when I was with my pride. The only ones I've seen have been with this pack, and..." He seemed to realize something. "They weren't wolves." His muscles bunched, tension building within him. "Tank is a bear and he..." Bronn's face shifted into a mask of disgust. "He finds women he likes, kidnaps them, and turns them, uses them, then... kills them as soon as they no longer suit him. And yes, they change, but I don't think it's because of being turned, but because they're forced to... by Tank."

My other hand balled into a fist, my jaw tight, teeth grinding. Something needed to be done about Tank. I'd seen the cold look in his eyes, people were playthings to him. And now, hearing Bronn speak of kidnapping, rape, and murder along with the man's complete lack of remorse, a rage burst to life within me. And the fact that Harley, the previous alpha, had made a man like that one of his betas spoke volumes about the sort of man he'd been as well, not to mention what pack life must have been like.

Venom laced my voice when I whispered, "There is no way I'll put up with such behavior in *my* pack." I swallowed a foul lump in my throat. "I don't know if I'll change when I turn or not, but I know that I won't be an alpha like you had before. I don't want to hurt these people. I want to take care of them... take care of you, Bronn. That's the sort of alpha I want to be. I won't stand for anyone in my pack hurting anyone else, whether they're in the pack or not."

A bundle of restless dread formed in my gut at the thought of what Tank had done, what this pack had been like, and what they'd all gone through. Also, I had no clue how I was going to stop men like Tank and Brick, nor change things, not yet. That only made that cold, hard ball in my stomach all the heavier. Yet at the same time, I felt some of the knotted tension within Bronn release.

"That's my hope," he said and the tremulous optimism with which he said it broke my heart once again.

Then he rose and turned, all serious strength. "If you truly become an alpha like that, then I won't just be your beta, everything I have will be yours." He knelt again like he had earlier today, looking me in the eyes. "My body, my mind, my soul, my life and..." His gaze on me intensified. "...my love."

He looked away immediately after saying that, so I don't know if he saw the shocked surprise on my features.

But I quickly convinced myself he meant love in a platonic, familial way, not romantic. That's all that made sense. One man falling for me, because of some strange fated attachment, was odd enough. Another man falling for me the same day, especially without any magical fated whatever? That wasn't possible.

Not for me.

Not for plain Jane Myers.

Still, I felt compelled to say, "Thank you."

He smiled, then nodded and rose to return to his station at the door.

I slid under the covers and snuggled into bed. Since it was still early, I pulled up a book on my phone. As fate would have it, the book I was reading was a reverse harem romance, featuring a sexy demon, a stalwart angel, a gruff vampire, and even... a werewolf. And the more I read, the more I began to fantasize about little-old plain-Jane me having her own hunky harem of guys. Only in my case they were all shifters with real names and faces and very sexy bodies. But that was just a fantasy...

...wasn't it?

BRONN

I wanted to believe Jane. Watching her sleep, so peaceful, with just a hint of a smile on her lips, I almost *could* believe it.

She'd be different.

She had to be.

But a roiling fear in my gut warned me not to trust anyone, and that feeling had been keeping me safe for years now. The only person I'd let myself trust was Tyson, and that had been after years of him proving himself. In my head, I couldn't fathom how this kind and gentle woman could become anything horrible. But then if she didn't, how could she beat Brick?

And that's how my thoughts circled all night. I wanted change, wanted Jane to be that change, but if she couldn't beat Brick, nothing would change. And if she did beat Brick, would she have changed too much? Forced to become something horrible to kill a horrible man?

After a while, I shifted into my lion form and lay

down across the doorway to rest. My keen ears would pick up anyone in the hall, or even outside the house.

Everything was easier in animal form. I was still me, but there was a simplicity to an animal's world view: food, rest, mate. Larger concerns lingered, but they seemed distant. It felt good to be in this form. Needless to say, it wasn't something Harley had allowed much. Even just seeing me, larger than the wolves, had scared them and that meant more assertion of their dominance. But now, tonight, I could stay as a cat and no one would care.

I heard a sharp gasp and was instantly alert. I raised my head and looked around to see Jane sitting up in bed, staring at me.

"Bronn," she whispered. It wasn't a question. It seemed like some confirmation to herself. Still, I nodded my large head.

My enhanced night vision caught the glimmer of her large eyes as she continued to stare at me.

"I…" She gave a little laugh. The sound was so light and free it pierced my heart. "There's quite a difference between knowing you're a lion and seeing it." She let out a shuddering breath. "You scared me for just a moment, but now… I feel safer, knowing you're protecting me." She smiled. And that too struck my heart.

I would protect her. I'd do anything for her. I'd only known her for a day, but I felt closer to her than I had to any woman, other than my mother or sisters.

I couldn't say if this was love, because I didn't know what love felt like. I only knew I'd protect her with my life and that I wanted to know her, be around her, touch her, comfort her, serve her. Something in her scent called to my soul. I didn't know if it was the mate-scent or not, but I suspected it might be. Yet she and Tyson were fated, so I had to stay away.

"Thank you," she whispered and smiled, then she lay down and returned to rest.

Just like that she'd accepted me for who I was, what I was.

And that made me want to care for her all the more. Suddenly, I wasn't sure if I'd be able to stay away from her. I needed to talk to Tyson.

When dawn broke and light began to filter into the room, I shifted back to my human form, dressed, and slipped out into the hall. Colt was there, standing, leaning against the wall between her door and the bathroom. He had his eyes closed, but they opened the instant I came out.

"Can you watch her for a moment, I need to find Tyson."

"Anything wrong?" Colt asked, concerned.

"No." Or at least I hoped not.

Colt nodded and, keeping the door to Jane's room open, he stood in the doorway, so he could keep an eye on her and the other doors along the hall as well. "Go."

I padded softly, as only a cat could, through the house, checking every open area, but Tyson wasn't inside. I slipped out the side door and caught Tyson in his wolf form just as he was coming around the corner of the house from the back.

Every wolf was different, their coloring varied, and I knew Tyson's well enough: dark charcoal grey — almost black — over most of his frame, but with a long brush of white along his belly, a lighter patch on his snout, and another flash of white in a diamond shape above his eyes.

He trotted up to me then nodded his head to indicate going inside. I went in, letting Tyson in, and only then noticed the pile of clothes on the kitchen counter by the door. He shifted back and dressed quickly, a habit we'd all picked up.

"What is it?" he asked, and I noted the concern in his voice. "Is Jane okay?"

"Yeah, she's good," I said, not knowing how to start this conversation.

He sagged with relief. "What do you need?"

I needed Jane.

That was the problem.

The only wolf that had ever been good to me was fated to the woman I was pulled to mate with. Fuck it, I'd always been blunt, a man of few words. I'd just say it.

"I want to mate with Jane." Then I quickly added, "Too. If she'll have me... if she'll have *us*... if you're—"

"I know," he said, cutting me off. "I could see it the instant you two kissed yesterday, when she bound us as betas. Something... changed for you."

"It's her scent," I said. "It calls to me, tells me she's my mate."

Tyson nodded slowly.

"I can't stop thinking about her," I added. "Something about her, that strange mix of vulnerability and strength... I want her more than anything."

He nodded again but remained silent.

"I spoke with her last night," I pressed. "She's so... different, caring and kind, and yet so resilient and determined. And... and when she saw me as a lion, she... she accepted me. Just like that." I didn't even know what I was saying anymore.

"Just because I'm fated for her doesn't mean I won't share her, if that's what she wants," Tyson said as if it were nothing. "Hell, it's not like male alpha's don't sometimes take all the women from the pack. If Jane wants more than just me, I won't stop her, and I won't stop you from pursuing her. I couldn't think of a better man to share her with."

"What about Colt?" I asked. "I'm pretty sure he sees her in a similar way." I'd caught his glances at her. They didn't seem to be on quite the same level as my desperate pull, but if Jane was open to multiple mates, then I was fairly certain he'd put his hat in the ring.

"Him too," Tyson said with a grin and a shrug. "It's really up to Jane. As long as I'm *one* of her mates I'll be happy."

I nodded. "Good, thank you, Tyson." That had gone a lot better than I'd feared it might. On to the next topic. "There is another thing I wanted to talk to you about."

"Oh?" Tyson said, open and encouraging.

"I know you. I trust you. You're the only wolf I've ever trusted. Most of what I've known of wolves is violence and pain. I... I need to know that Jane is not going to become like that." He sighed, about to launch into a long speech it seemed, but I went on quickly. "But I don't know how she'll defeat Brick if she doesn't become a monster like him. Tyson, I don't want her to change, but I can't see how she'll win as she is. Please just tell me turning won't make her different?"

He let out another sigh and waited a moment. "You done?" he asked with a bit of a laugh. "You and I were both born this way," he whispered to me. "I have no clue what it will do to her. But Nico would know. He was turned twenty-some-odd years ago. He'd probably remember. And I know Harley and the betas were nothing but cruel to you, but the rest of our pack would have had your back, if they were able. They're mostly good folk. Harley ruled with fear. Jane will liberate them. I think you'll find you have more friends than you realize. But if you don't feel comfortable talking to Nico, I can talk for you."

Nico Juarez was an older man, husband to Dana Juarez, who was a natural born wolf. From what I understood of their story, they'd met in their twenties and she'd eventually told him what she was. He'd asked to be turned and they'd lived happily on their own for a while, having a son. Then Harley had found them and made them part of his pack. The only reason Nico was still alive was because he was a non-dom and had instantly deferred to Harley, which appealed to the man's ego. Nico seemed like a decent person, but I still didn't trust him. Yet perhaps Tyson was right and I should start giving some of the others a chance.

"I'll talk to him," I said. "Thanks Tyson... I don't want her to change, but..."

My friend laid a strong hand on my shoulder, squeezing slightly. "I know. I fear the same thing. I don't want her to become something she's not, but if she doesn't, then will she be able to defeat Brick? I don't know, but I hope we can find some way to make that happen." He blew out a heavy breath. "But that's for after she's turned. For now, I'll talk to Colt... about that other thing, make sure we're all on the same page. You go talk to Nico. I hope that eases your mind."

I nodded and we parted ways. I headed into the basement.

At the base of the stairs Kira, in wolf form, kept watch over the others down here. She nodded to me, letting me pass and I skirted the room. Most of those here were still sleeping, but Dana Juarez was up. She came out of the basement bathroom, naked. Most of us slept naked, ready to shift if needed.

As I'd told Jane, nudity didn't mean much to us... though, seeing Jane last night had been something entirely different. With the scent of her arousal — the sweet-heat of nature after a summer storm — filling my nose, suddenly her naked form had been... incredibly stimulating. She may not have been young and taut and tight, but that didn't matter. Her mature, womanly form, with full breasts and hips and thighs had aroused a primal lust within me, and my cock had turned to stone.

I blinked away that pleasant memory, returning to myself.

"Dana?" I whispered, so as not to wake the others.

She turned to me, unashamed of her nakedness. For a moment I found myself comparing her and Jane, since they were about the same age. Dana was a handsome enough Latina woman, with black hair and tanned skin. She was a bit more athletic of build, breasts and hips smaller and higher, but then she was a wolf. As much as I had no clue how the turning changed a person mentally and emotionally, I knew there were definite physical changes. The effects of aging were slowed a little and one became stronger and tougher, healing quicker. Dana had been a wolf all her life, so she looked younger than her age. Still, I wasn't aroused looking at her. She was just another naked wolf. Whereas even just the thought of Jane made my arousal stir once again.

"Bronn?" Dana asked, voice even, her powerful presence pushing me.

My warring dominant and non-dom sides fought to figure out how to react to her. She was a dominant and might have been an alpha in other circumstances. I tried to quell my mounting fear. She wasn't threatening me, just being who she was. She went to her small bundle of things on the floor and began dressing.

"I'd like to talk to you and Nico about his experience turning. I want to know how he felt after. You knew him before and after and might be able to provide some insight as well. I want to know how much Jane might change after she's turned."

Dana nodded, curt and precise. "Fetch my mate and we'll talk." She returned to dressing.

I went into the guest room and found the three men inside already waking and tidying up the space. It looked like the two younger males, Lucan and Jake, had shared the bed. Nico had slept on the floor.

"Nico, can we talk?" I asked.

As a non-dom, he instantly deferred. "Yes, of course." He dropped what he was doing and came with me, half dressed in pants only. When he came out into the rec room, it was curious to watch his behavior. He kept his gaze averted from any other women and headed straight for his mate. He bowed his head to her. She offered a cheek and he kissed it lightly.

"Sleep well?" she asked, the first to speak.

"Yes, my love," he said grinning widely. "You?"

"Carpet is better than a forest floor, no rocks, but... it doesn't feel right."

"Of course, my dear."

"Now, come, let's not keep our new beta waiting. Why don't we speak in here?" she suggested, motioning to the third door off the rec room, which led to an unfinished utility room.

Once inside, the two of them looked at me, waiting. The cold concrete floor must have been hell on Nico's bare feet, but he didn't complain. It was hard to reconcile that I was technically superior to Dana now. She was a dominant type and trying to defer to me, but all my years in the pack had taught me to stand down from a powerful presence like hers.

I steeled myself and asked what I'd come to ask. "I am curious how the turning will affect Jane. Nico, you were turned. How did you change?"

Nico looked at Dana. She nodded, giving him permission to speak. "Other than the ability to shift, I didn't notice a lot of changes, not right away, but there were many. I'd never been an assertive individual and that was enhanced as a wolf. I became a non-dom and had to learn what that meant. Turning takes who you are and... stretches it." He grimaced. "It makes you even more of what you were before. If you were scared, you're more scared. If you're strong, you become stronger. As much as

I did get physically stronger, that didn't seem as big a thing as all my personality traits being enhanced and amplified."

I nodded at this and looked to Dana for her perspective. "Anything you noticed?"

"I know he may have felt that things changed significantly, but for me, they didn't. He simply became more... himself. I'd chosen him for all of his traits, so when they were enhanced, I didn't really notice it as much as he might have." She smiled. "Yet, I *did* notice his enhanced physical traits. When he mounted me, he was stronger and surer. He's always sought to please me, but now when I asked him to be harder, he can be. It's very satisfying." She spoke of their sex life as if giving directions, dispassionate. Nico, however, blushed.

Dana finished with, "Also... he smelled different, though I suspect that is not the sort of change you are concerned about."

"And, what do you think of our new alpha?" I asked. "Given what little you know of her so far, will she be dominant or non-dom?" If she was non-dom, there would be little chance of her winning against Brick.

Dana considered for a long moment.

"May I?" Nico asked. She nodded to him, a curious expression on her face.

"She faced down Harley," Nico said evenly. "And that may have been only a protective instinct as a mother, but I tell you this. Even with everything he'd done, I'd never once considered standing up to the man. I can't say for certain, but it seems to me there is at least some dominant in her."

I nodded to this, as did Dana, and she added, "Watching her yesterday, she was confused and not in her element. I think she's scared, but also strong enough not to let that fear control her. I can't say for certain which way she'll go, but I feel my mate is right. There's at least some dominant in her."

That was good. I'd seen it too, flashes of her strength. Yet I'd seen a lot of vulnerability as well. I sighed. "Thank you both. I hope she'll be a strong alpha and lead us for some time to come."

Nico nodded.

Dana gave a bland smile, her eyes still hard. She had reservations.

I left them and headed back upstairs.

My heart did a ragged dance in my chest, surging with hope and falling with fear in equal measure. I hadn't gotten the solid answer I'd been hoping for. I'd learned that Jane probably wouldn't change much after being turned, she'd just be more of who she already was. I was happy for that. But if she couldn't become as fierce as she needed to be, then her reign as alpha would be short lived. And the thought of losing her so soon after finding her terrified me more than anything in my entire life.

JANE

I woke to the sounds of people moving around the house. Usually, I was the first one up.

Were Izzy and Milo up before me? For a moment, I was confused. Then all the events of the previous day flooded back to me, overwhelming me for a moment.

I'd killed a man.

I lay in bed, blinking, unable to comprehend this strange new life of mine.

I was alpha of a pack of biker werewolves. Though some were bears and others were... lions.

Lions.

I recalled the huge form of Bronn as a lion laying by my door. I'd seen lions in zoos, but Bronn had been larger than any of them. He'd looked so powerful and yet so at ease, like some housecat lounging on the floor, just hundreds of times larger, and I was grateful he was on my side.

Slowly, I sat up, a hand to my head, trying to stop the headache I could already feel coming.

"Hey beautiful," came a purring voice from the open doorway. I blinked and saw Colt standing there.

I instantly pulled the covers up over myself, not because he was looking at me, but because the door was open. In truth, I really liked the way the young man was looking at me, even if I didn't understand why he'd look at me that way.

"Oh, sorry," he said, brow furrowing. He glanced out into the hall one last time. Noises from around the house let me know people were up and moving even though it wasn't much past dawn. He nodded to someone in the hall, then closed the door as he stepped in.

"That better?" he asked.

"Thank you," I said. "I just need a shower and—"

The sound of running water as the shower came to life in the bathroom next door stopped that thought. I blew out a breath and got up, wrapping a housecoat around myself.

Glancing at Colt, he was still giving me that *best-friend-who-could-be-more* look, even once I was bundled in a heavy terrycloth robe. And before I'd covered myself he hadn't been staring at my tits. That's what men generally focused on. I had a plain face and features, but a significant bust. Most men's gazes slid off my face and headed right to my breasts, but not Colt. And for some reason that made sense. That look he gave me held a certain respect, the *best-friend* part of it.

Someone knocked on the door, and I shifted closer to the far wall where I wouldn't be seen if it opened, then I nodded to Colt.

He asked who it was through the door, Tyson

responded, and the large man let Tyson in, then winked at me and slid out of the room.

"You're not dressed," Tyson remarked instantly as his gaze traced over my entire body. The heat of his dark-blue eyes instantly stoked my own inner fire, and my cheeks warmed.

"You should get dressed," he said quickly, swallowing hard.

It was clear that wasn't what he wanted, and I knew it. Because I wanted it too: both of us naked on the bed with his cock buried to the hilt inside me.

My nipples hardened to aching points, ever-so-sensitive to the brush of the cotton fabric over them. The blistering heat inside me seemed to press down and my folds were suddenly wet and ready for that imagined situation.

Tyson's nostrils flared.

Last night Bronn had smelled my arousal, something about *summer rains*, and I got the feeling Tyson was getting a good whiff of me now.

I had to stop getting wet at the mere thought of this man, especially if he could tell.

Wait... if he can tell and Bronn can tell then... oh-my-God, everyone can tell!

"I need a shower," I said quickly, forgetting the shower was occupied. "Then I'll get dressed."

Tyson grunted. "Tank just got in the shower with Petra. He'll probably use up all the hot water before he's done."

"Then I'll go downstairs," I said. There was a shower stall in the downstairs bathroom. I strode toward him and hoped he'd get out of my way. He didn't. I stopped in front of him, hands clasped tightly over my robe. I couldn't decide if my tight grip was to keep it closed or in anticipation of tearing it off.

Tyson nodded. "Get what you want to wear," he said, voice low, eyes raking over me. "If you're naked under that robe on your way back from the shower I'm not sure I could control myself."

Wow. I had to press my legs together to contain myself at the thought of Tyson tearing off my robe and having his way with me on the basement stairs.

I swallowed and turned away, quickly gathering what I'd wear for the day, then Tyson escorted me down to the basement bathroom. The door was locked.

"Ginny's in there," Kira said as she finished dressing, slipping her leather vest on over her short-sleeved shirt.

Tyson swore.

"Is that bad?" I couldn't remember which one was Ginny.

"She doesn't like you," Tyson explained. "She was Harley's girl and had power, now she's got nothing. She's probably not coming out until she's used up the hot water. Unless you want me to break down this door."

Cold shower or broken door. A door could be fixed. Or... I could wait a few hours to shower. But I had a feeling I wouldn't have a lot of time today to just wait around for things. I sighed. "Break the door."

One swift kick and it burst open. He stalked into the small bathroom.

"Out!" he barked at the woman in the shower. "Our alpha needs the shower and she comes first!"

"Screw her," came the woman's deep voice. The

mottled glass of the shower stall kept her mostly hidden from us.

"Out or I force you out," Tyson said, opening the door to the small shower stall. The woman inside was many things I was not: tall, leggy, blond, with a straight nose and full pink lips. Her bust was roughly a match for mine, but far perkier, and she looked at least ten years younger than me. Tyson glared at her, but I was fairly certain he wasn't looking at her the same way he looked at me. The fact that she was naked didn't seem to mean anything to him, and I had to keep reminding myself that nudity wasn't a thing for them.

"Fine, *beta*," she snarled the word. "And fuck you!" She didn't bother to turn off the water before storming out. She glanced at me as she marched by, giving me a derisive scoff before parading over to the couch to begin dressing. Right. Well now I knew how I'd remember which one was Ginny: Stuck-Up Barbie.

I went into the bathroom, which was a mistake, as that forced Tyson to brush past me on his way out of the tight space. We both paused as my chest pressed to him and the stiff bulge in his pants pressed to me.

I saw the battle in his dark eyes for that split second, whether to leave me or tear off this robe, lift me onto the pedestal sink and fuck me. And I didn't know which I wanted more.

The moment vanished as he regained control of himself and kept going. "I'll be outside," he growled, then closed the broken door as best he could behind him.

I hurriedly undressed and stepped into the shower, but I didn't wash myself immediately. I needed to get

Tyson off my mind. I reached down and rubbed my clit as my other hand — as if it was his — roamed over my chest.

Like last night, it didn't take much before I was shuddering with a release. Also like last night, it was only barely satisfying.

After, I quickly washed myself, scrubbing hard to get *that* scent off me, even as the water began to cool. I forced myself to stay under the spray as the waters turned icy, hoping that would cool what I was feeling. I didn't have time to be horny, I had a pack of wolf-bikers to rule.

That thought sobered me enough to get out and get dressed.

Time to start the day.

COLT

THE MORNING WAS CHAOS. A HOUSE THIS SIZE WASN'T meant to hold this many people. Hot water couldn't return fast enough, both toilets clogged up... several times, breakfast was a feeding frenzy, and the old betas made everything worse.

Tank forced Petra to strip and bent her over the dining table while the rest of us tried to eat in peace. Jane wanted to leave, I could see it, but Tyson stopped her, whispering something. He was probably telling her this was just another test and leaving would only give dominance to Tank. So Jane stayed, but she couldn't eat and she just kept staring at Tank who stared back the whole time.

After Tank had finished with Petra, he wouldn't let the pregnant woman eat either, which I think got Jane's motherly instincts in a knot. Her jaw clenched so tight it twitched.

A few moments later, Ginny returned from taking food out to Brick. The big, shit-eating grin on her face told me she'd done something foul. It took me a moment before I smelled it. The smell of breakfast and scent of all the others around me had occupied my senses, but now...

"Fuck," I whispered to myself and got up, running back down the hall. I followed the scent to Jane's room and I knew, even as I opened the door, what Ginny had done. The bitch had pissed all over Jane's bed.

That led to a shouting fight between Jane and Ginny, which ended in Ginny being banned from the house, like Brick.

Bronn and I hauled her outside and dumped her on her ass. Tyson came out a moment later with her things. But still, she grinned. She knew she'd won that round.

Jane got the kids off to school and the house mostly settled, but she was still full of barely suppressed rage.

"Take her for a walk," Tyson told me. "Calm her down. Do what you have to. I don't want to turn her like this."

"What I have to?" I asked with a single brow raised. I lowered my voice for the next part. "Does that include what we talked about earlier?"

Tyson had told me about Bronn's interest in Jane and their thoughts and concerns about multiple mates. I'd told him I definitely wanted to be a part of that... as long as that's what Jane wanted.

Tyson glanced over his shoulder at Jane, then back to me. He wore the oddest smile. "Yeah, it does. And gods, I wish I was you right now, but I don't think Jane and I are ready for what might happen if we were left alone together." He sighed, clearly craving her, but restraining himself. "Distract her, however she needs. I'd prefer if she was in a good mood when I turn her." There were myths and legends about how a person's emotional state when turned could flavor their entire life as a shifter. I was pretty sure they were just myths... but then why risk it.

I nodded to Tyson, then went to Jane. "You look like you could use a break. Let Tyson and Kira take care of things for a bit. Come for a walk with me. There's something I want to show you."

"All I want to see right now is Ginny's head on a pole!" she hissed.

"I know, but trust me, this will be good," I said with a bit of a laugh. "Come on," I urged, and she sighed, then relented, and let me escort her out of the house.

It was a beautiful early fall day, warm and bright, some of the leaves just starting to change. I pointed her toward the park and forest off the dead-end loop of her street.

Jane huffed and grumbled, tense and upset as we walked. The park had been where the pack had left our bikes and kept our things at night before we'd met Jane. The marks of our bikes still marred the green lawns.

She marched beside me, silent, as we headed past that and into the wood, but I knew she was still struggling with her roiling emotions. They tainted her scent. She smelled more like dried grass and sunburn. Also, like I had the day before, I felt her rage physically, like a heat on my side. She was a powerful little woman.

I wanted to touch her.

"You mind if I...?" I reached out and laid my hand tentatively on her back, rubbing slightly.

She sighed and seemed to melt into my touch a little. "No."

I rubbed her back for a bit as I led her through the trees, then switched to her shoulder, eventually pulling her just a bit closer to drape my arm around her, rubbing her arm. It felt natural to have her leaning against me like that. She tilted her head to rest on my upper arm, the top of her head roughly level with my shoulder.

"Why...?" she breathed. I sensed uncertainty ripple through her. She didn't know how to go on.

"Just say it," I whispered.

"Why do I feel so comfortable around you? I shouldn't. I hardly know you and you're a huge man who I certainly shouldn't have gone into the woods alone with, but..."

"I'd never hurt you, babe," I whispered. "For one, you're Tyson's mate, and I'd never do anything to hurt him. But also... you're..."

How did I tell her how I felt? That she reminded me far too much of a woman I'd once loved who my father had killed just to spite me.

She huffed a breath. "Just say it," she echoed my words from a moment ago.

Fuck it, why not. "I was in love a while back. She was older than I was, but I didn't care. She thought she was plain and unattractive, but she was beautiful to me. She didn't care that I was all busted up inside. She loved me anyway and that... that meant everything to me. I felt comfortable with her, like nothing I'd ever felt before. Then... she died." I sighed. Jane didn't need to know the horrific, gory details. "You remind me of her. Something in your soul, how kind and caring you are... and that look you get, like you're not worth anything, even though you're a wonderful, beautiful person."

She stopped walking and I was forced to stop with her. Turning, she looked up at me, confused. "Do you really mean that?"

"Every word," I said softly.

"You've only known me for a day," she whispered.

"Doesn't matter. I saw how you stood up to Harley to protect your own. I see how you want to help Petra, even though you don't know her. You didn't have to take us into your house, we could be camped on your lawn, but you did. You care for your kids, which to you probably seems mandatory, but it definitely isn't in my world. I don't need to know everything about you to know you've got a good heart, that you're kind and loving and generous and passionate and strong."

She stared up at me for a long moment, her eyes searching mine. I felt like she could see my pain, the knot of rage and resentment in my soul.

"Two days ago, I thought you were all ruffians and brutes," she said slowly. "But you and Bronn and Tyson... You've protected me, helped me, spoken softly and gently to me." She shook her head again. "Tyson and I are fated, and you and Bronn joined him as my betas, but... Why? Why would you do something like that? Because I look like some woman you used to know?" Her brow furrowed again. "And why do I feel so safe around you? I really shouldn't."

I swallowed a lump in my throat. I wasn't sure exactly why she felt safe around me, but I was very glad for it. I'd spent my life trying to be everything my father wasn't, but in a gang like ours, that wasn't easy. I'd had to be a brute at times. I'd hurt people at the command of my alpha. But I'd hated it, where my father had reveled in it. Perhaps that was what she was sensing?

"I've been forced to be a brute," I whispered. "But I never wanted to be. I want to be like you. And now that you're our alpha, I guess... I'm allowing myself to finally be who I want to be. I know you won't command me to hurt an innocent person, but I'm certainly willing to defend you against another brute, if needed. You're a good person. I couldn't protect other good people in the past, but I can now. I don't know, maybe that's what you're feeling from me?"

"Maybe it is," she said softly. "I don't know." Then she breathed a laugh. "I wish talking to Tyson was this easy."

I smiled at that off-hand compliment. "It's the fated thing. It messes you both up. Got you thinking more about fuckin' than talkin'."

Her eyes went wide, then she laughed again. More and more of the tension she'd been holding was draining out of her. "You've got that right." She shook her head. "How did one as young as you get so wise?"

"I may be young, but I've seen a lot of shit. That either breaks you or makes you tough... and wise... I guess."

She put both her hands on my chest over my leather cut, gazing up at me. I couldn't help myself, the pain and confusion in those soft brown eyes made me want to hold her. I brought my arms around her softly, gently, and she leaned into me. I choked up for a moment at how easily she melted against me. I didn't quite understand it, but I wasn't going to question it. I had a wonderful, caring woman who wanted to be close to me and I didn't want to screw this up.

We stayed there for a while, me holding her softly while she rested against my chest.

Finally, she asked, "What did you want to show me?"

"A few things, and we're almost there, you wanna see?" I asked, excited.

She nodded against my chest.

I let her go and we walked side by side again, but this time she took my hand. I held her soft palm in mine as we walked. I couldn't help but grin at how easily she'd accepted me. It was her large heart, and I'd never do anything to break it.

I loved everything about this woman. So what if she was a decade or more older than Tasha had been? Her body might not be fit and firm, but hey, soft curves were good too. And really, it was her heart that called to me. I felt like I'd found Tasha's soft soul once again in Jane.

The brush and trees gave way to the rocky fringes around a burbling brook. I loved the peace and serenity of this place.

"There." I pointed to a large flat boulder to one side of the rocky stream. "That's one of the things I wanted you to see... or rather... feel."

"Feel?" she asked as I drew her over to it, our hands still together.

"Yeah," I said. "There ain't nothing better than lying on that rock in the sun."

She smiled. "That does sound nice."

We'd reached the rock and I released her hand to

climb up. It was tilted slightly, easy to get onto and also perfectly facing into the sun. I lay down and closed my eyes and let the sun's heat wash over me.

"Like this," I said.

I heard her move and felt her lying down beside me, then... a long sigh of contentment.

"Ohhhh, this *is* nice," she said softly.

I opened my eyes and rolled onto my side to look at her. She smiled faintly, narrow lips spread, the lines on her face easing. She looked like some goddess of nature with her hair splayed out behind her, her eyes closed peacefully, and her rounded chest rising and falling evenly.

"I want to kiss you," I said, then blinked at myself, surprised I'd said it out loud. I'd certainly been thinking it.

Her eyes fluttered open, blinking at the sun shining down on her, and she raised an arm to shade her face. An aroused curiosity lit up in those soft brown depths, but also confusion and uncertainty.

"Colt..."

"Yeah, I know, sorry, forget about it." What had I been thinking?

She gave a soft laugh. "I mean I'm flattered that ah... a nice, *younger* man like you would be interested in a plain older woman like me. But—"

"No, Jane. You're not plain, and you're not that old." There was a mild reprimand in my tone that I couldn't hold back. I couldn't bear it when kind souls like her — and Tasha — put themselves down.

"I dye my hair, that makes me look five years younger... most days." She grimaced.

"Just don't think of yourself that way, okay? My... the woman I knew, she did the same thing, putting herself down, saying she wasn't pretty, but she was... and so are you."

Jane blushed. "Thank you, Colt. And I mean, it's not like I don't want to be kissed. I do, or part of me does, but ah... well..." She swallowed. "I'm still getting used to everything that's happened and... and now suddenly I'm fated for Tyson, and... I don't even know what that means. But if I'm... going to someday be with him, then... I don't think..."

Gods, she was cute when she was flustered.

"Being fated to Tyson doesn't mean you can't kiss me," I said softly. "You're the alpha, you can do whatever the fuck you like. Alpha's having multiple mates isn't uncommon. Usually, they take and keep them by force, but I get the feeling you're not like that."

She shook her head with an appalled expression.

"But if you did want multiple mates, then you should know that Bronn and I are also interested. We've talked with Tyson and he's good with it if you are. We're perfectly happy to share you, if it means we get to be with you."

A glimmer of expectant hope flickered in her eyes. "But Tyson and I are fated, and..." It was clear she didn't know much about that.

Neither did I.

"I don't know all the details, but from what I understand, being fated is just between you and your fated and doesn't mean you can't have others." I went out on a hopeful limb. "I get the feeling you wouldn't complain if Bronn and I wanted to mate you along with Tyson?" I lowered myself enough over her that I was shading her eyes.

She let her arm fall away. Her cheeks flushed a bright, hot red, and I could hear her racing pulse.

"Do you?" she murmured.

"Want to mate you?" I replied matching her whispered tone. "Hell yeah. But for now, I'll settle for a kiss."

"Oh..." she said, her voice breathy.

"But I won't, if you don't want it."

I didn't know how long we stayed like that, eyes locked, with me bent close over her. I wanted to give her space to refuse while letting her know how much I wanted this. But perhaps I was crowding her too much. I began to pull away when she whispered, "Wait!"

My heart leaped and began racing. "Yeah?"

"I... I don't know what I want. I don't know what to think, but I know I like you being here, close and..."

I smiled. "Don't think, just feel. What feels right?"

She closed her eyes for a moment, her chest rising as her breathing grew heavier, the flush on her cheeks deepening. "I just want to feel... I want..."

I had a suspicion of what she wanted, but she wasn't allowing herself to feel it, to say it.

"Just tap me if I go too far, and I'll back off," I whispered, then leaned further over her, putting a hand on the rock on the far side of her to keep from rolling onto her completely.

I gently lowered myself until my lips brushed over

hers. Her eyes fluttered open, shocked but not upset, and I let my lips press to hers again with a bit more force.

Almost instantly, she gave a shuddering sigh and relaxed into the kiss, her eyes closing again.

I kept my eyes open, wanting to see her pale skin and splash of dark hair, even if it was way too close and blurred. She tasted so amazingly sweet, like honey. I kept the kiss light, playful, mouths closed. I'd take my cue from her.

Her hand came up to my face, cupping my cheek, caressing. I'd shaved last night before going on watch, having suspected things would be a mess this morning. My cheek was smooth and so was her hand.

And when, with just the slightest push, she signaled for me to withdraw, I did.

Her lips were parted as her eyes blinked open to stare up at me.

"Sometimes," she whispered, her voice faint, "I think this is a nightmare. Other times... it's like a dream, full of wonders I can't quite believe. Like this." Her brow furrowed again. "Do you really find me attractive?"

Her doubts and fears were palpable in her tone and expression, and it made me want to crush whoever had told her she wasn't the most amazing woman in the world.

"Yeah," I said. "You were married, right? Didn't your husband ever tell you how amazing you are? Or how lucky he was?"

She blushed again. "Only when he wanted..."

Yeah, I could fill in *that* blank easily enough. "Then he was a moron."

She gave a bit of a laugh, then sighed heavily. "I've had a lot of time to think about it, and I think he only married me because I had nice tits and I'd go down on him occasionally." She turned her face away, clearly embarrassed, looking toward the stream. "He left ten years ago. I'd suspected he'd been having an affair for a while, ever since Milo had been born, but I hadn't known the details. Then, when he left, I heard there was a twenty-something woman at his gym who'd vanished at the same time."

"Yeah, fucking moron," I whispered. "You're so much more than a hot body. I knew it the moment I saw you. The moment you protected your kids and stood up to Harley, then with how ashamed you were after. I could see you had a soft soul, but one that was strong enough to fight for what's important."

"Do you mean that?" she asked, rolling her head back to look up at me.

"Every word."

"Even the hot body part?" She seemed skeptical.

"Yeah, that too," I chuckled, leaning down and brushing her lips with a kiss again before drawing back. "Why don't you tell me which part you think isn't hot and I'll tell you why it is."

She flushed even more, her breath coming in heavy shuddering gulps. She licked her lips, her pink tongue darting out, and I had to restrain myself from diving into her mouth to catch it. "My breasts are—"

"Perfect?" I finished for her. She gave me a sour look so I went on. "Natural, round, heavy and full, a handful. I just want to hold them and kiss them and worship them until you think they're the best things in the world."

"Oh... wow..." She gasped. "But my thighs—"

"Are perfect too, strong and smooth and beautiful. I want to feel them wrapped around me, hugging me tight, or perhaps pressed against my cheeks while I taste their hidden treasures."

She swallowed, trembling, tears around her eyes and heat painted on her skin. The next one seemed harder for her to say. "And... my... stretch marks?" she asked, curious.

I smiled. I'd seen her belly that morning after she'd gotten up, wearing that sexy sleep outfit of a sheer cotton top clinging to her breasts and otherwise naked down to her yoga pants. Yeah, there was a slight pouch around her bellybutton with the faint white lines of stretched skin scars around that. But frankly, after two kids, I thought she looked amazing. I wasn't sure if she worked out or not, but her waist actually curved in, not out, giving her a pretty stunning hour-glass figure.

"Yeah, I've seen 'em, so what? I assume you work out, cause if you don't, then you have one hell of a metabolism. You still have a nice waist and..." I moved my hand from supporting myself to brushing over her belly. "All I see is the natural beauty of someone who's brought life into this world. I've got scars too and you don't think I'm ugly, do you?"

"No," she said. A tear escaped her eye and ran down the side of her face into her ear before she could blink it away. Yet her voice was heavy with self-contempt when she said, "But I bet your previous girl didn't have big thighs or stretch marks."

"She hadn't had kids yet, so no stretch marks, but she did have a bit of a soft belly and nice round thighs." I smiled. "She also had a small chest, always complaining she couldn't quite fill an A-cup. So, yeah, you're different, but *you* are no less beautiful."

I could see her reservations, the doubt behind her eyes. So, I'd show her. "Don't think, just feel, remember?"

I lowered myself to kiss her again. Her receptive lips opened to me this time. I let my tongue dive into her depths, tasting her. Gods, she tasted so damned delicious I couldn't help but moan softly into her mouth. My hand on her stomach slid up to her breast and gently took a handful of her softness into my palm. I massaged her softly, feeling the lacy pattern of her bra through her shirt.

Then it was her turn to moan into my mouth. It was the sweetest sound I'd ever heard. Yeah, she may have been a decade or more older than I was, but I didn't care. She was everything I wanted, a perfect reincarnation of Tasha's tender soul in a mature and womanly body. I wanted her with all of my scarred heart, and I intended to show her just how much I wanted her, and how beautiful she was.

JANE

I COULDN'T BREATHE, BUT NOT IN A BAD WAY. IT WAS MORE that my mind had completely stalled out, stunned and overjoyed that a guy like Colt found a plain-older-woman like me beautiful. My brain was so fried I couldn't quite remember how to inhale and exhale.

But also... I didn't care.

I was lost in all the wonderful sensations Colt elicited. His firm lips pressed and his tongue delved and explored my mouth. His large hand knew just how to trace my breast, how to cup and press and knead. I was far too warm and wondered how much further the two of us would go if I took my shirt off. I didn't know if it was his attention, or the sun beating down on me, or Colt's earnest words, but I was boiling like lava and loving every moment of it.

I wanted this so desperately even though I'd fought it. But Colt was right. When I'd turned off my mind, all I'd wanted to *feel* was *him*. It wasn't logical. It didn't make any sense. I shouldn't be making out with a man I hardly knew, but I didn't care anymore. He made me feel incredible and I didn't want him to stop.

"Even if you weren't my alpha, you'd be in control," he murmured between nibbles on my lips. "You tell me what you want and you'll have it." His lips kissed my chin and along my jaw, back to my neck. "Or, if you aren't the instructive type, then just say stop if I'm going too far, and I will."

God, he was so considerate and kind and gentle... and huge and powerful and manly, an exquisite combination.

The trouble was I didn't know what I wanted.

No, that wasn't true.

I knew what I wanted. I was just terrified to ask for it.

After having spent a day with Tyson and the pull of our strange and powerful fatedness... after two semi-satisfactory orgasms, trying to scratch an itch I couldn't quite reach... after *all of that*, what I really wanted was a mind-blowing orgasm.

Except I wasn't the type of woman to demand orgasms. So, I'd do as he suggested and let him keep going until I wanted him to stop. Maybe somewhere in there, I'd get something, or I'd get brave enough — or desperate enough — to ask for it.

He hitched a leg over one of mine, sliding it up between my thighs until his knee pressed softly against my core.

I moaned again, and without his mouth over mine, it seemed far too loud out here in— I blinked and froze.

"Wait...!" I gasped.

His lips, which had kissed their way down to trace the collar of my long-sleeved shirt, pulled back instantly.

"What's wrong, gorgeous?" The way he said "gorgeous," low and breathy, made it clear he meant it. It wasn't just some random pet name, and it made my insides melt to hear him think of me like that.

"We're just... out here... in the middle of nowhere," I said, frantic.

He smiled. "On my favorite rock. I think it's going to be my favorite for a completely different reason after this, though."

I sat up, arms tight around myself, even though I was sweating and panting with sweltering heat. "But it's so... exposed. What if someone came along?"

"Then they'd see a sexy woman being pleasured by a younger man," he replied, sitting up next to me. "I wouldn't blame them for wanting to watch. I could watch you all day and all night. Also... no one comes out here, especially in the middle of the day. There are no trails back here and we're far enough out of town that only your neighborhood knows of these woods and most of them don't go that far into them."

All very logical and sensible things, but still... I felt like I was on display for the entire world to see.

"Trust me," Colt said, slipping a large hand to my back and rubbing comforting circles. Except his heated palm only made my steamy-state worse. "I'd rather be doing this on your bed, but..."

My bed... right.

Ginny.

I blinked. I'd been furious with her not that long ago but now... "Is that why you're doing all this? To make me forget about what happened?"

"A secondary reason, yes. The primary reason was I wanted to be alone with you, touching you, pleasing you."

"You were doing very well on both fronts," I whispered.

"But you don't want to continue?" he asked as his hand on my back swept up to move my hair aside so he could kiss the back of my neck. It was a long, sensuous, lingering kiss, that turned all the skin above my waist into gooseflesh and drew another soft moan. God, I wanted him.

"If you keep your bra and panties on, it won't be any worse than being in a swimsuit in public," he whispered.

Despite my reservations, my mind had been looking for any loophole, any excuse to keep going with Colt, and his swimsuit reasoning made sense enough for me to finally relent.

"Done," I breathed and whipped off my shirt.

"Hell yeah... gorgeous."

Again *that* word from *his* lips filled my core with dripping heat.

Suddenly my jeans were way too hot, and I reached down to tug them off when Colt stopped me.

"Oh no. Let me." Even as he said it, he removed his shirt and leather vest with one fluid motion, revealing a thick, muscular torso.

I already knew his arms were huge, though not as chiseled as Tyson's. It seemed the rest of him was the same: big, thick, and beefy.

Yeah, that was the word: beefy.

Everything was heavy and rounded. And though he

was big and beefy, still there wasn't an ounce of fat on him. He was all muscle, just thick powerful muscle instead of finely honed chiseled muscle.

And yeah, he did have scars, lots of them. Most were old and faded, but it was clear he'd had a rough life. Then, there were his tattoos.

I usually didn't go for a man with ink, but on him, it looked *good*. I'd already seen the ones on his arms. Down his left arm was a swirling stylized pattern which integrated parts of a bear: roaring maw, claws, and sad eyes. His right shoulder held the image of a wolf, a lion, and a bear, overlaid and integrated. The one I hadn't seen before was the profile of a bear's head on his chest. It was stylized, more outline than detailed, but the eye of the bear was a tank and from its mouth out ran a stylized horse: a *colt* escaping a *tank*.

Colt laughed. "Ah... gorgeous? You're drooling."

I licked my lips and yup, there was just a bit of drool at the corner of my mouth. And I wasn't even ashamed of it.

I reached out and ran my hand over the tattoo on his chest, feeling the twitching hard muscle beneath.

"Wow," I breathed.

He smiled. "Thanks. I think the same of you." I found that hard to believe, but I couldn't deny the hungry look in his eyes. "Now, lie back and let me take those jeans off."

I did as he instructed, the sun-warmed stone against my back was nothing compared to the wildfire within me. I was quickly becoming a sweaty mess, but I didn't care anymore. A juicy beefcake of a man was about to take my pants off and that was all I was thinking about.

He leaned over me, his lips picking up where they'd left off at the base of my neck then progressing lower onto the exposed flesh of my cleavage. Meanwhile, one of his hands deftly popped the button of my jeans. Something about that quick release made my core clench and pulse with need.

I lost my mind for a moment once again, going completely by feel. Hard lips pressed to the soft flesh of my left breast. My zipper slipped down, and thick fingers traced over my panties. A searing kiss landed between my breasts, his tongue lapping up the puddle of sweat there, and he rumbled with contentment, like I was the sweetest thing he'd ever tasted. His hands pulled on my jeans and I lifted my hips as he slid them down. Then I set my hips down and lifted my legs so he could remove the heavy fabric entirely.

He removed my flats one at a time as he kissed my belly. That made me squirm, I didn't like the thought of anyone seeing my stretchmarks, let alone... touching them. But then I turned my brain off again, going back to how it felt, and I had to admit, it was amazing!

Another kiss, lower, just above the hem of my panties, sent heat spiraling through me. He finished taking off my jeans, then his strong hands shifted me, opening my legs as he moved between them. Supporting my butt and thighs, he easily lifted me and kissed my panties over my folds. I let out a clipped cry, pressure making me instantly soak the soft cotton. Another kiss on my apex, longer, savoring, then he set me down and settled his heavy body over me. He kissed my breasts again as he lowered himself to press against me, a heavy bulge in his jeans crushing against my clit.

I let out a low, throaty moan, rocking my hips to move myself over that hard ridge behind his jeans.

And that was it, I couldn't stand the teasing any longer.

"Orgasm," I gasped.

He gave a laugh. "That's not usually what most women yell when they're having one."

"No... want one. Please!" There. I'd said what I wanted and I was too worked up to care.

"One orgasm, coming up... unless one isn't enough?"

Oh God! I'd certainly take more!

But I was gasping and breathing too hard to say it.

His lips found mine as his full weight settled on me for just a moment. It was brief, and uncomfortable with the stone beneath me, but it was also primal and hot and made all the more divine by the imperfection of discomfort.

Then he lifted away, his lips staying, but most of the rest of him leaving, rolling to the side. I wanted to roll with him, keep that gloriously hard ridge against my clit, but his strong hand on my side pushed me back down. Then that same hand slid over my hips and in to my center. He flicked my clit three times, still over my now soaked panties then pressed the tip of his finger firmly against me, slowly rubbing, sending shivers rolling up and down my body.

That alone almost made me come. Colt certainly knew how to use his hands.

With a soft swipe, his fingers pushed my panties aside

to press and play in my dripping folds, and a deep throaty moan escaped my lips. He drank it up with his kisses, and I trembled, my need building higher and higher.

Finally — finally! — someone's fingers other than mine were touching me, and it felt amazing.

He traced my wetness up to my clit and circled it, playing for a moment as my hips rose with need. He easily pushed them back down and slid his finger back to my weeping opening, slowly pushing it inside me.

Oh, God. Yes!

My eyes rolled back, my back arched off the stone, and I let out a whimper just as his lips lifted away from mine.

His tongue ran over my mouth for a moment before he whispered, "You're amazing."

Then he shifted, his other hand pulling down one side of my bra until my breast popped out. He captured it with his mouth, sucking and licking my already taut nipple into an aching bud.

I moaned. *So close!*

Colt pushed a second finger into my folds, stretching me, then curled them up hitting my G-spot while grinding the base of his palm over my clit. It took just one rocking plunge of those strong fingers and the rough rub of his palm to make me scream and buck and come.

Oh, yes!

Oh, yes yes yes.

This! This was what I'd wanted. This glorious, mind-aching, body twisting, muscle-straining orgasm was everything I'd hoped for and more.

And he kept me going, his hand rocking over me, his

fingers slowly plunging into me, while his lips made my aching tits feel twenty years younger. I was a sweaty, messy puddle by the time I came down, still steaming hot, lying on that rock, struggling to catch my breath.

"That," Colt grunted as he withdrew his fingers, "was fucking hot." He licked my juices off his hand and groaned. "You're fucking hot."

JANE

STILL DAZED FROM THAT EVER-SO-SATISFYING ORGASM, I was hyper-aware of Colt next to me, groaning, shifting, clearly uncomfortable.

"Need a hand-job?" I asked, stunned at myself for even asking. I wasn't the sort of woman who said things like that!

"Nah, gorgeous." There was that word again, sinking silky warmth into my gut. "I'll take care of it. You rest."

He rose and was quickly out of his jeans. His cock, which rocketed up to attention, was like the rest of him: beefy, strong, and thick.

He staggered off the rock and down beside the river. I rolled my head to watch him as he pumped himself, grunting and trembling. All the while, his eyes were on me, drinking me in. Just thinking about how aroused I made him, got me hot once again. I reached down to stroke my still tingling clit.

"Oh yes, fuck!" Colt cried out, watching me tweak myself.

He came, long shots of ropey cum streaming out into the river, and I guessed he hadn't had a release in a while, because his orgasm seemed unending, long enough for me to rub out another body-shaking orgasm of my own. It seemed my own fingers worked well enough... when I had some inspiring stimulus right there, standing before me.

When he finished, he leaned on the boulder where I lay, gulping air.

Wow. Just... wow.

That was one *virile* young man.

And he wanted me.

Me!

When I looked at Colt, I didn't feel the instant, primal need I felt with Tyson, but in some ways, this was better. He hadn't been forced by fate to be with me. He wanted me for me. I didn't understand it, but I wasn't going to question it anymore. All I knew was that bed or not, I wanted to get Colt alone and get his huge cock inside me... some time when I wasn't exhausted and a little sore. Apparently, even just two of his thick fingers inside me had been a little too much. I hadn't had anything inside me for a while... a long while. Apparently, I'd need some practice.

With Tyson, our fatedness would probably preclude anything slow and easy. It might be nice to have another option. And it seemed like I'd have *two* other options? Colt had mentioned Bronn might also be interested in being with me.

Wow.

My mind couldn't quite comprehend all this attention. Tyson was fated for me and I knew at some point we were going to crashed together in a primal frenzy. Colt thought me sexy exactly as I was, which was a minor miracle. And Bronn also wanted to be with me?

Perhaps I shouldn't be surprised, given how Bronn looked at me, like I was some tempting dessert he wanted to gobble up.

So...

What the fuck, why not? My life was getting turned upside down. I might as well enjoy some part of this.

Still though, having sex again after a decade meant my mind may want it but my body wasn't ready.

Colt easily vaulted onto the boulder again, clearly comfortable being naked, his semi-aroused cock flopping around. He stretched out next to me on his side, and his eyes roamed over me hungrily, even after he'd gotten himself off. It reminded me I still had my panties pushed over and one tit out.

I began to put myself away, when he offered, "I could splash you with some water. You seem... *really* hot."

I chuckled. "I am." I knew he didn't mean sexy. Though it did feel a little empowering to admit I was "hot." And a splash of water sounded divine. I knew it would probably be better if I took my underwear off, but I still wasn't ready for that. "Yeah, sure. I—"

I yelped as he knelt then scooped me up, as if I weighed nothing. He carried me off the boulder, then set me down lightly on my feet in the river. The chilly waters reached up to my ankles and felt divine after my body had become a furnace of desire.

"Actually, if you wanted to splash yourself, I had

something else I wanted to show you while we were out here."

More? "Oh?"

He laughed. "Yeah, the rock was one. What we did on the rock was two. And three... well it's something I can't do easily while indoors."

"Okay?" I said, curious. "Go ahead."

I crouched in the shallow, rocky stream and scooped up the cool water, dousing myself over and over as Colt moved away. He walked backward, his steps sure as he watched me with a grin. When he was about twenty feet from me, he winked and...

His body tore itself apart and reassembled.

It was quick — seemingly painless — and when he was done, there was a massive, hulking bear where he'd been.

For just a moment, I froze, terrified. People weren't supposed to be this close to bears, especially bears *that* big! This was one of those massive *one-swipe-of-those-huge-claws-will-take-your-head-off* type of bears. Then he gave a whuffing sound and shook himself and somehow that broke the spell on me. It almost seemed like he was smiling as he ambled over to me and nudged me softly with his broad, flat face.

I reached up and stroked his thick, soft fur, and he made a noise that sounded half-way between a growl and a cat's purr and pressed into my hand. I scratched harder, and he gave a contented huff then sat next to me in the river, splashing water everywhere, making me laugh.

So *this* was a werebear. No— They called themselves shifters... right? A bear shifter?

Bronn was a lion shifter and Tyson was a wolf shifter... though I hadn't seen him as a wolf yet, only that strange half-wolf-half-man thing.

That got me thinking. "Do werewolves—" I quickly corrected myself. "Do wolf shifters look like wolves when they change?" I asked. I was going to be one, so I should know.

Colt-the-bear nodded.

"But Tyson... I saw him as a sort of wolf-man-thing."

Colt nodded again. Then he got up and ambled away a bit and shifted again. This time it took a bit longer and looked a little more painful. The clearing filled with the strange thousand-bones-breaking noise I'd heard with Tyson. And when he was done...

I gasped, eyes wide.

His bear had been terrifying, but this form... this half-man-half-beast form was truly horrifying. He was as big as the bear, but seemed larger still because he stood on two thick legs, and his arms were massive affairs ending in those same huge claws. His head was that of a bear, but facing forward and a bit lower, sunken into his mountainous shoulders. There was a more feral and dangerous quality to this form and thankfully, he didn't stay that way for long before returning to his human self, which again took a moment and sounded painful.

He shook himself, as if that form made his skin crawl, then strode back over to me, still completely naked and all the more glorious for it.

"Yeah, we have a mid-way form, a hybrid beast-man, that we can use. It's harder to get into and harder to stay in it, but it's far more dangerous than either of our other forms. All the agility of a man and all the power of a beast." He crouched next to me and put a comforting hand on my back, stroking me softly. "Sorry if I scared you."

"You did, but I... I had to see that, I think." Then, as if teasing that thought out to its logical conclusion, I asked, "I'll have to become one of *those* to face Brick, won't I?"

He nodded. "Yeah, probably. Sorry." He pulled his hand from my back and began splashing the cool water on himself. "Now that he knows you've got a gun, he'll be ready for that. He'll shift as soon as the challenge starts. Bullets don't affect our hybrid forms as much. We hardly feel the pain. And something tells me you're not a crack shot, that you got lucky with those shots on Harley, didn't you?"

I didn't want to think about it, but... "Yeah. Never used a gun before that. I only bought it a week ago after..."

He grunted. "After we attacked the man down the street?"

"Yeah."

Another grunt. "That was... unfortunate... and all Tank's fault."

I knew a bit of what had happened and knowing it was Tank made all the more sense. Apparently, one of the bikers — Tank — had seen Carrie Pearson leaving her house and harassed her, getting a little too close, blocking her from getting into her car. He'd apparently said something about taking her into the woods to be with a "real man."

She'd been terrified, of course, and screamed. That had

caused her husband James to come running out to try to defend her, which had earned him a sound beating. James Pearson had been in the hospital for three days and still looked rough. I didn't know the Pearson's well, they'd only moved into 109 at the end of the cul-de-sac a few months back, but talk was, they were thinking of moving out now.

It hadn't been the only altercation with the gang either. The Herrera's in 107, had also had a few run ins with the bikers. Elena was pregnant and there'd been some shouted comments about "sharing some milk" and things along that line. Hector, her husband had been pushed around a bit as well, but the thing with the Pearson's had been the worst altercation so far.

Colt sighed. "Brick's going to know you a lot better at the end of this week, and he'll use everything he can against you. He knows he can't let you just have the pack."

"Why can't he?" I asked heavily. "Why can't he just get on his bike and leave?"

A chill shivered down my spine. The water I'd splashed over me had done its job and my body had cooled, so I went back to the large rock and pulled on my shirt. Then I hopped up onto it and sat. I'd let my feet dry before I put my jeans and shoes back on.

Colt sauntered over, his cock swinging heavily, slapping his thighs. God he was impressive, and sexy as sin.

He pushed a hand back through his blond hair. "Brick knows that if he leaves now, most of the pack won't go with him. Tank and Sonny would. And Tank would take Petra. Ginny would probably go with him as well, but that would be it. He'd be an alpha with no pack, which is no real alpha at all."

"This is all so he can assert himself over those people again?"

"Yup. It's all about control. And if you don't want that to happen, you have to win against him."

"Can I?" I asked, voice cracking. I swallowed hard, trying to clear my throat. "Is there any way I can win?"

Colt sighed as he hoisted himself up to sit on the edge of the rock beside me. "I can help train you. It won't be much since we only have a few days, but Tyson and Bronn and I will make sure you're as ready as you can be."

Somehow, I didn't think that was going to be enough. I didn't ask the other question on my mind. *Does it have to be me who fight's Brick?* Something told me that Tyson, Colt, or Bronn would be jumping at the chance to take my place if they could.

"We should get back," I said, then shivered. Except now I wasn't cold, I was terrified. Going back meant being turned, and from what Tyson had said, it wasn't going to be pleasant.

Colt nodded.

We lingered a few moments longer, drying ourselves, before dressing and heading back through the woods.

Before we reached the edge of the forest, I grabbed Colt's hand. He stopped, smiling down at me.

"Yeah, gorgeous?"

I really did love that name. "Just... thank you. For showing me the rock and... everything else. Thanks."

I've never felt this beautiful and sexy before in my life.

His smile grew, stretching wide.

"Anytime," he purred. My core shuddered and my thighs clenched with all the heavy implication he threw into that one word.

And I was going to take him up on that offer. If I only had a week to live, I might as well have some steamy, mind-blowing sex before I went.

Still, I couldn't give up, couldn't think about failure. My kids — and the whole pack — were on the line, and I couldn't let them fall under Brick's rule.

I didn't know how... but I had to win.

JANE

WHEN I RETURNED TO THE HOUSE, I FOUND TYSON WAITING for me with bandages and a sharp knife laid out on the dining table. I smiled despite what I knew was coming. My time with Colt had been a wondrous awakening, and I still felt a little giddy.

That, and as a bonus — not to mention a minor miracle — the guys had managed to get Tank and Sonny out of the living room, so we were alone.

"You can do this, gorgeous," Colt whispered as he dipped close, sending a thrill through me. "You're stronger than you think."

He kissed my cheek and headed back out, something passing between him and Tyson just before he left, some wordless communication.

"He'll make sure we're not interrupted," Tyson said as I sat at the table. "Are you ready?"

I drew in a long breath and looked from Tyson to the others in the front room with us. Bronn leaned against the wall where the back hall met the front room, and Kira leaned on the counter in the kitchen. Their faces were somber, serious.

I steeled myself. This was it.

I was going to be turned.

Tomorrow I'd be a werewolf.

My life had already changed so much in such a short time and it would change so much more in the next few hours.

I swallowed my fear and nodded to Tyson. "I'm ready," I said, sounding tougher than I felt.

I tried not to look at Tyson. That was dangerous territory. Colt had just reminded me what it was to be sexy and desired, and the look in Tyson's eyes promised more of the same. I may have been a little sore, but something told me that wouldn't matter. If Tyson and I lost control, our fated nature would make sure my body was ready for him.

"Hold out your left arm," he said.

I did, and he took it in his large hand, holding it steady as he rolled up my shirtsleeve.

"I'm going to cut you here," he said, tracing a finger over the inside of my forearm about a third of the way from my elbow to my wrist.

I shivered with the contact, that one touch tingling through my body to sizzle in my core.

"It's going to hurt," he continued, his tone brusque, and I knew — even though I wasn't looking at him — that he wasn't looking at my face either. We were both far too primed, and we had to get through this without any impromptu sex. "Then I'll cut my hand and place it over your cut. That will hurt too, since I'll be applying pressure to make sure our blood mingles. After that, Bronn will bandage us both."

I nodded.

"I boiled this while you were gone, nice and clean," he said as he raised a sharp kitchen knife. "On the count of three, count with me. One."

"One." My anxiety spiked, twisting into a writhing ball in my stomach at the anticipation of pain. I'd be a mess by the time we got to three.

"Two."

"Two—ow!"

He quickly slid the knife across my forearm. Pain burned through the limb, drawing a yelp and making me jerk against his grip.

Tyson held tight.

"What happened to three?" I demanded, blinking back tears.

"Better this way." He actually chuckled a little. Given how I'd felt, he was probably right.

My gaze started to flicker up to his, but I yanked it back to the knife, watching as he cut his palm before clamping his hand over my arm.

We both gave a grunt of pain, and I clenched my teeth.

"How long...?" I forced out.

"Not long," he replied sounding like he wasn't bothered at all.

My gaze flicked up again, I couldn't stop it. Pain filled his eyes and somehow, I knew it wasn't for what he was feeling, but for what *I* was going through. Then our gazes met and all the pain in his eyes vanished, replaced by desire, a rush of heat flushed his tanned skin.

A corresponding wave of fire swept through me and suddenly every part of me was sensitive and raw. Oddly, I felt hardly any pain, overwhelmed with too many other sensations. Just the brush of my clothes over my skin sent sparks of shivering bliss through me.

Tyson's eyes grew hungry, feral. He lifted his hand away then grabbed my arm with his other hand and lifted it, dipping his head to lick my wound, lapping the blood away, never taking his eyes off mine. The wet heat of his tongue seemed to soothe my wound while spiking my pleasure and I almost moaned. I pressed my thighs tight, my core aching and churning with need.

"Excuse me," Bronn said softly, breaking the moment.

My lust faded and the pain returned.

Bronn quickly placed a heavy gauze pad over my cut, then taped it down. He did the same for Tyson, then proceeded to wrap my arm with bandages.

"From what Nico told me, that's going to burn and itch," Bronn said. "We'll keep it wrapped up for a bit."

I nodded.

"You'll also feel warm and faint, a bit feverish, but not too bad, mostly just weak and tired." He looked to Tyson. "You clean up. I'll take her to bed."

Tyson growled, nodding.

I looked over at Kira. "Could you come along?" I asked. "I'd like to know everything you know about being fated."

Kira nodded as I rose.

I didn't even make it one step before Bronn scooped

me into his arms, carrying me down the hall to my bedroom. I wasn't sure I wanted to be in there after what Ginny had done, but when we got there, my bed was gone, replaced with the one from the spare bedroom downstairs. I hadn't asked for that but wasn't sure I could undo things now. The bed would be nice, even if I felt ashamed of taking it away from others in the pack.

After my talk with Colt, I'd been trying to force myself to think of all of these people as mine, under my protection, my... family. That meant I wanted the best for all of them, like I did for my own kids, so taking a bed away from them didn't sit right with me... although I suspected they wouldn't take it back either.

Fine. I'd accept this for now, but I'd make sure we got a new bed, perhaps a lot of new beds, in the near future.

Bronn laid me down, still fully dressed, and stepped back as Kira sat on the side of the bed. The pain in my arm was fading, a lethargy sweeping over me, and I guessed she noticed as she skipped any preamble and spoke swiftly.

"I don't know a lot about being fated," she said. "I only have memories of what my grandmother told me."

Fair enough.

Still, even second-hand information was better than no information.

"My grandmother knew because her parents had been fated. It's actually very rare, but — for reasons nobody can discern — it tends to happen more often in certain bloodlines of wolves, older ones...like mine." She grimaced. "In most cases, it affects the male first. They experience a moment of disorientation, usually while looking at the female in question, then they just know they have to be with her. Again, the legends vary, but often, when the male touches the female in question, she's... infected, for lack of a better word. Sometimes this doesn't happen and in those cases the male... ah... well, he either takes her by force or goes mad."

"Oh." Suddenly I was glad I'd been infected. I didn't really want to contemplate the other options.

Kira sighed. "No one really knows why it happens, it just does. Then the wolves in question just need to... live with it. Those that embrace it can have very satisfying lives. Those that fight it... well, they either go mad or are just miserable."

Right. Don't fight it.

Tyson had said he'd been restraining himself until I was a wolf. Though he'd also said that once I'd shifted, we'd need to focus on my training in combat. Could we hold out for the entire week? It had only been two days and the pull was already incredibly strong. Something told me a week was going to be far too long to wait.

"Thank you," I said to Kira.

She rose but paused at the side of the bed. "He's a good man. Under all the horrors and gruesome life lessons Harley inflicted on him... he's a good man." I didn't know who she was trying to convince, me or herself.

"I know," I said softly, and she left.

Bronn returned to kneel at the side of the bed and whispered, "I'll stay with you."

I smiled at him, feeling another, heavier wave of fatigue sweep through me. I didn't think I'd last much longer before passing out. "What else can I expect, when I turn?"

"As we get closer to moonrise your fever will intensify. That cut will also hurt like hell. Then the moon will rise and you'll shift into a wolf. It's going to hurt a lot."

"I won't become a beast-man-thing?"

"No, just the animal. You'll be hungry and want to eat. Ideally, we'd let you run in the woods, hunt, find game and eat it. That's more satisfying, more natural. But moonrise is early in the day this month, it'll still be light out and I know you don't want your neighbors seeing a wolf running down the street. So, when I was shopping yesterday I got an assortment of raw meat." He gave a laugh. "I cleaned out two different butchers to get enough for you and the rest of the pack. Most of it was for you. Once you're sated, you'll rest and recover. Then, when the moon sets, you'll shift back. That should be less painful than the first time, but probably still... not comfortable. You'll be tired for most of the next day, and that's it."

"Then you and the others will teach me how to fight?"

His face grew grim. "Then we'll teach you how to fight."

My eyes closed for an extended blink. I was fading fast.

"Rest," Bronn said. "I'll be right here."

And knowing that made it easier to close my eyes again.

TYSON

I'D DONE IT. I'D TURNED JANE.

I'd taken a caring and wonderful woman and cursed her.

It was unforgivable... but necessary. She needed to be the one to fight Brick.

The grinding ache of my fated attraction to her sung out with the knowledge that she'd soon be a wolf and ideal for mating. Even now, with my hand still stinging, the desire to be with her was near to overwhelming. I wanted to run into her room, rip off her clothes, and ravish her.

But I didn't.

That was the reason Bronn was with her now instead of me. Luckily, I had a task to help keep myself busy. I'd promised Jane I'd talk to the pack: let them know they were free and ask what they wanted for their lives now. I had no clue how they'd react to such a thing, but I hoped, for Jane's sake, they wished to be free as much as I did... even if they didn't know what that looked like.

I waited for my mom to return from Jane's room, then pulled her aside. "Got a sec?"

"What is it?" she asked, sounding curious as we made our way into the basement. We stopped in the corner at the bottom of the stairs. Not too far away, Dana and Nico Juarez were giving some lessons to the youngest members of the pack: Winnie, Lucas, and Jake. There were old, ratty textbooks and papers scattered on the basement floor.

Since none of us had ever seen the inside of a normal school, the best we could do for our pups were lessons taught by elders, using out-of-date, scrounged-up textbooks.

"Jane has a rather simple, but radical idea about the pack," I whispered so I wouldn't disturb the lesson.

One of my mom's brows rose.

"She wants to know what we want out of life, for ourselves. She'd rather be an alpha who sets us free to live the life we want, instead of us giving her the life *she* wants."

My mom shook her head slowly with a heavy sigh. "Brick is going to eat her alive."

"No," I said firmly. "He won't. I'll teach her how to fight and survive. But if — no — *when* she does, she'll rule this pack and rule it her way. So, I figured I'd ask you first. What would your ideal life look like?"

Kira sighed, running a hand up her face then combing her fingers through her silver-streaked hair. "I have everything I want. I wanted kids, and I got them." A half smile spread on her lips. "I couldn't be prouder of you. Rita's headstrong, and in the wrong pack that might get her hurt, but for now it's serving her well, and I wish Brutus wanted more for himself, but he seems happy."

"And you like taking care of the other pups," I said. She'd become a pack-mother of sorts to all the children.

She nodded. "And there are two more now, Jane's kids. If she doesn't survive Brick, I'll make sure they're safe."

"You don't want anything more?"

She grimaced, an expression which said, *yeah, I do, but it's silly for our kind to want such things.*

"What is it?" I urged her.

"I mean, I could do with a little peace and quiet." She looked around, her gaze landing on the kids on the floor. "I wouldn't mind if we had better materials to teach the pups. I also wouldn't mind if there were more pups around, but I sure as hell ain't gonna be the one having 'em." She sighed. "And if we're going to stay here, we'll need more room. Being stuck in this basement is okay for a few days. It's out of the rain and it's warm, but we'll go crazy if we have to stay down here indefinitely."

"See," I said with a grin. "I knew there were things you wanted. There's probably more too, if you spend some time thinking about it. Just give it a try and let me know what comes up, okay?"

"And this alpha bitch will magically make it all happen?" Kira asked, skeptical.

"I don't know. It depends what people want. I get the feeling it will be a process, and we'll all probably have to pitch in to make it work."

My mom shrugged. "Just don't get people's hopes up."

That would be the hard part. "Yeah, I know."

Next, I interrupted the lessons and asked everyone there what they wanted. The youngsters weren't much help. Their answers revolved around simply *doing* whatever they wanted, not necessarily *having* anything permanent.

When I asked Dana and Nico, she did most of the talking. "Freedom to come and go as we please, to say what we want, and live our lives in peace."

Nico nodded at this.

"Do you want to keep your bikes and that lifestyle?" I asked, curious. There was a part of me that would miss the open road.

Dana thought for a moment, seemingly uncertain.

Nico asked, "Might I?" And she nodded to him. "Most shifters are bikers or nomads of some sort mostly because they don't have any one place to call home, yes?"

I nodded.

"And from what I've heard, this dates back as far as people can remember. Our kind was persecuted, chased out of villages, and so on. We formed packs for protection and kept on the move so no one would find out what we were. Also, if we didn't have a home, no one could take it from us. The world would be our home, something like that, yes?"

I nodded again, curious where he was going with this.

"But, has anyone really checked to see if that's still the case?" he asked earnestly. "When I found out about your kind, when Dana told me what she was, I was curious and uncertain, but I wasn't afraid of her, I loved her. Perhaps we could find a home here? If we're going to change our ways, perhaps this small community might accept us... if we are kind to them and so on. I, for one, would love a bed to sleep in every night."

Dana gave a hum of approval. "He makes a good point. It would have to be done strategically, mending the fences within this community before we come out, but it might work. Then we could have a home, a real home, finally."

A part of me really liked the idea too, though with the things we'd done to some of the people around here, that fence-mending wasn't going to be easy.

"Anything else?" I asked.

"If we are going to stay, we'd need..." Dana proceeded to list off everything that was wrong with this current location. I summed it up in my head as: *if we're going to stay here, we'll need a bigger place.*

After that, I spoke with Cassie, a mild-mannered woman who was relatively new to the pack. Her story was an unpleasant one. Our crew had come across her and her husband and their teenage son a couple years ago. Harley had killed her husband and taken her and her kid into his pack. Harley had claimed her as his mate for a while, before Ginny got jealous and reasserted herself, after that Cassie had been mostly left alone.

It took some coaxing to get Cassie to say anything, she was used to keeping her mouth shut and doing what she was told. When she did, all she really wanted was a safe place for her son — Jake — to grow up.

When I spoke to my sister, Rita, I was a bit surprised to find out that she liked the open road and didn't really want to settle down. Yet, she agreed that having a sort of base that she could return to, wouldn't be bad.

Last was Brutus, my brother. He just wanted to be a wolf and do wolf things, hunt, sleep, and mate.

All in all, it was fairly unanimous that people didn't really want to go back on the road. Which also meant most of the pack would support Jane and not want Brick to win the upcoming challenge. I took that as a favorable outcome and went to see how Jane was doing. After being away from her for a while, I felt a bit more settled. There wasn't the savage need to rut with her, just a desire to be near her.

She slept, with Bronn diligently watching over her. He said he'd get her some water and a bit of food for when she woke, then left to gather that while I took over his post.

Oddly, seeing her like this didn't seem to trigger my mating instinct. Perhaps it was our eyes. Whenever our gazes met, we both seemed to go into some sort of heat. I kept wanting to have some time with her, just to talk, to get to know her more, to understand this strange woman who was now my alpha and my fated, but that never happened. One look at those soft brown eyes and my mind shut off and my body took over, surging with need to be buried inside her, pleasing her, claiming her.

But right now, I had a moment to just appreciate her. I stroked her hair. It was so soft and full, wavy and thick. I'd always preferred darker hair, closer to black, like my own, but Jane's was a perfect dark golden brown with highlights that shifted between silvery and sandy-brown. I could get used to hair like this, so soft I just wanted to bury my face in it.

An image flashed in my mind of our naked bodies

sliding together, me behind as I pressed her to a wall, all of this wonderful hair in my face as I filled her, eliciting heavy moans and whining cries.

The vision faded and I took a deep breath. Apparently, I didn't need to see her eyes to slip into that heated state.

She shifted and sighed, her eyes fluttering open. Her skin was warm, but not overly fevered yet.

"Tyson?" she whispered.

"I'm here." And for what seemed like the first time, I looked her in the eyes and wasn't overcome with lust. She looked so vulnerable, and my urge to protect and care for her outweighed my need to fuck her. "Bronn is getting you some food and water." She hadn't had lunch and would probably be hungry.

She smiled up at me and everything clicked into place inside me when I saw that delighted expression. All I wanted was for her to be happy, content, relaxed, satisfied. This was another side of being fated it seemed, wanting your partner to have everything they needed and desired.

"Thanks," she said, a bit dopey.

Then she stretched, arms out, body arching, and the way her clothes moved over her, straining over her tits, was too much. I rose and turned away, hiding the painful bulge trapped in my pants. I resisted the powerful urge to rip the clothes off both of us and have her. It didn't help that she still vaguely smelled like sex from her time with Colt, her scent now rich with the aroma of steaming grasses after a summer's storm.

I was glad he'd given her what she'd needed, just as I

was fairly certain what she *didn't* need was someone ripping off her clothes and ravishing her.

Bronn returned and the moment passed. My arousal slowly faded as he went to her and helped her sit and eat some food.

I shook my head. Our situation — all three betas being enamored of our new alpha — felt both right and also... bizarre. Most alphas had betas and most alphas took more than one mate. But most alphas *weren't* women whose betas *were* their mates. It wasn't unheard of, just very rare. My mom knew tales — more like legends passed down from mother to daughter — of alpha females and their harems of men.

Luckily, my fated pull only demanded that I please and serve and care for my mate, not to have her all to myself. I'd be happy as long as she had everything *she* needed. If she needed Colt and Bronn, then I'd gladly share.

I paced the room, still fidgety, until Bronn had finished helping Jane eat. He winked at me as he left with the dishes, mouthing the words *talk to her!*

Yet, when I returned to the bedside, Jane was sinking down under the covers, her eyes kept closing in extended blinks. She needed more rest, so instead, I sat with her, stroking her hair again.

"That feels nice," she breathed, her voice distant. Then, whether she was dopey with sleep or perhaps beginning a bit of a fevered delirium, she whispered, "Fated... my fated... fated Tyson, my beloved... dark and handsome and yummy." She made a humming sound as if she'd eaten something delicious.

Just hearing those words on her lips, even if they were from a nearly insensate state, made every part of me tingle with pleasure.

"I'm here," I whispered. "For whatever you need. Forever."

She made another happy humming sound then settled and slept.

I huffed a soft laugh. If anyone had told me two days ago that I'd be soothing some woman, feeling all sappy and lovey-dovey for her, I'd have ripped them a new one. That definitely hadn't been me.

And the strange part was, I liked this new me better than the old one.

Now, I just had to help Jane survive so I could keep being this new me and not go mad with grief from losing her.

JANE

Things grew... fuzzy.

Every time I woke up, my room and the people around me seemed less and less solid and out of focus. I was feverish, I knew that much, and I had moments of lucidity, but more and more I just felt like a dizzy lump.

I could tell people apart by their voices. Tyson was gruff and gravelly. Colt was young and energetic. Bronn was smooth and silky and low. He came with food now and then. I drank whatever he put in front of me. Water was suddenly the *best* thing I'd ever had, cool and refreshing against the oppressive heat roaring within me. There was broth and bread, but not much more. I began to crave meat. I'd never been one for red meat myself. I preferred chicken or turkey. But right now, if someone had hacked off a chunk of cow, I would've devoured it.

Along with my appetite and temperature, my emotions were all over the place as well. Strange fever dreams mixed with memories. I relived shooting Harley over and over, shaded with a dozen different emotions from fear to rage to joy. That last one was confusing and strange. In my dream, I'd laughed while I shot him over and over, giddy and ecstatic, then I woke from the dream queasy and unsettled.

Luckily, there were other, far more pleasant dreams. I relived my time with Colt that morning. That dream also played out in many different ways. Sometimes I played coy and demurred, others I took charge and straddled him, riding him like a stallion.

In other fantasies, Bronn woke me with a kiss or a caress, then undressed me in bed and loved me gently until I was a mess of wet, moaning bliss. Oddly for these ones, half the time he was a lion, and that didn't seem to bother me at all.

Then there were my dreams about Tyson. If the others were steamy fantasies, then these were straight-up erotic brain-porn. We'd rip each other's clothes off and he'd take me in all manner of positions, half of which were only possible in dreams, I was sure. But in every position, in every blistering encounter, we were savage and wild with each other. We bit and clawed, screamed and howled, rough-fucking, hair-fisting, mouths spewing filthy curses that would make a sailor blanch.

"Jane." The voice was distant, but it was Tyson's. It was odd, like he was whispering filth in one ear and calling me softly in the other. "Jane? You... you're calling my name."

"Tyson!" I moaned. In this dream, his rough hands dug into my hips. His thighs slammed into mine, his hips punishing my ass as he drove his savage cock into me from behind. I was aching for him, face down, clawing and tearing at the sheets as he ripped a brutal orgasm from me.

I let out a savage grunting sound then screamed, "Yes, fuck me, you monster!" And when I looked back, he was the half-wolf I'd seen, snarling down at me as he pumped into me relentlessly.

"Jane... you're dreaming," the half-wolf said, just a bit too clearly.

Oh yeah, I was!

"She's dreaming of you, it seems," said another voice, Bronn's. Then a soft laugh. "Maybe you should get in there with her. Seems like she wants you."

Oh, Tyson was *in there* so very deep, driving me toward yet another body-clenching orgasm.

"Yes!" I hissed. "More. Harder!"

"We need to get her clothes off," Tyson said, exasperated. "It's getting late and she can't be dressed when she shifts. That would only complicate things."

It seemed quite odd for the savage wolf-man behind me to say something like that. Wasn't I already naked?

"Let me help," Bronn said. Tyson lifted me until my back was to him, and there, naked in front of me, was sweet, broken Bronn. He was gentle, kissing and caressing softly as Tyson continued to ravage me from behind. Somehow, they were both inside me and it was magnificent, one soft and slow and sensuous, the other hard and rough and brutal.

"Jane, if you can hear me, try not to move too much."

I wouldn't move a muscle. Trapped between these two amazing men, I was more than happy.

Warm, rough hands slid under my shirt... I was wearing a shirt?

No, I was naked already.

But I was also wearing a shirt.

Yeah, dreams were like that.

My arms were forced up as the shirt came off, Tyson grabbed my small wrists in one hand, capturing them above me while Bronn tenderly kissed my breasts, savoring them as Tyson... removed my bra?

No... wait. Where had the bra come from?

It didn't matter.

I moaned as somehow Bronn had his lips and hands on my breasts at the same time and I nearly came at the intense sensation.

Then hands were pulling down my jeans and panties. That definitely didn't work if two men were already inside me.

The dream faltered and my eyes snapped open.

The fantasy of my dream remained dancing before my eyes, but I could also see the hazy vision of Tyson over me, shifting my pants off.

God, I wanted him. No, I *needed* him!

I rose up and threw my arms around his neck and raked my teeth over his jaw in a savage bite.

I heard the deep, rumbling growl of contentment from him as he paused, my jeans and panties at my calves.

I licked his ear and released him with one hand, so I could grab his arm and force it between my legs.

"Claim me, you savage beast," I grunted into his ear.

"Fuck," he hissed as his fingers shifted over my aching, soaked pussy. "She's so wet!"

His thumb circled my clit as two fingers drove inside me, curling up and...

I came with a growling roar of pleasure. My mouth shifted down and I bit into his neck. I tasted blood, hot and sweet.

"Now your cock, I need your cock!" I screamed.

"No," he growled and his hand left my folds, leaving me cold and bereft.

I let out a long keening whine and began to thrash. I succeeded in kicking off my jeans and I quickly swiveled around to wrap my legs around Tyson. The hot throbbing bulge in his jeans pressed against my clit, and I rocked my hips over it, needing to feel him inside me.

He gave a grunting-roar. "Gods! I can't do this! Help me Bronn or I'll do it, I'll take her and it won't be soft and gentle. I don't... She doesn't know what she's doing. Please!"

"Please," I echoed. I was so close to another orgasm just from rubbing my clit on the rough fabric over his rock-hard cock. "Yes! I need you! Need your cock in my pussy!"

Tyson grunted a feral, "Yes!"

His cock swelled. His hands slid up to squeeze my soft breasts and there was nothing gentle about it. He'd probably leave bruises, but I didn't care. It was exactly what I'd wanted. I screamed through another release, spreading all my hot wetness over Tyson's jeans.

Hands moved over me, pulling me, shifting me.

"Just relax, sweetness," Bronn whispered. "You'll get enough of that later."

Yeah... I would. I was the alpha and I'd demand orgasm after orgasm from my betas until we were all limp and exhausted.

"Fucking hell! Fucking hell! Fucking hell!" Tyson breathed the words over and over. He sounded farther away now.

Dreams fully consumed me again. This time it was Bronn and Colt who were sandwiching me between them, all exploring hands and hard bodies. I snuggled down and sighed as they worked me over until I was a contented puddle of goo. Then they fed me meat, raw and bleeding, while still caressing me. What could be better?

"I think she's settled again," Bronn said.

"Thank the gods!" Tyson sighed. "I... fuck. I'm gonna need a new pair of pants."

Bronn laughed. "It seems our alpha can be a naughty little vixen, even if only in her dreams."

Oh yeah, I could! I was one hot mama and I wasn't afraid to show it... or was I?

Things got confusing again after that. Dreams of food and sex and hunting and running and bad bikers and good bikers all mixed together. I lost myself once more.

Yet, deep in the back of my mind some part of me knew what I'd done to Tyson, and I wasn't sorry for it in the least.

COLT

THE AFTERNOON DREW ON. JANE GREW MORE AND MORE feverish and lethargic. I had a few chances to check in on her, but mostly my job was to patrol and keep the house safe.

All too soon, the sun set, and I felt the pull of the moon about to rise. It was nearly time.

I did a final check on Jane. She shifted and moaned in bed, asleep, but clearly uncomfortable. Tyson stayed with her, he'd help her through the shift, when it came. Bronn leaned on the wall outside her room in case he was needed. I nodded to them both, then left for another patrol.

I slipped out the back door in time to hear the rev of engines. Brick gave me the finger as he revved Harley's old Road King. Ginny was wrapped around him and giving me a sour look as well. Brick let the bike loose and it dug a half-foot-deep hole in the lawn of the back yard before disappearing around the side of the house.

I followed them, just in case they were planning

something, but the bike quickly left the cul-de-sac, heading out onto the main road and away. I didn't trust those two, this night of all nights. Them leaving was just a little too convenient, but perhaps I should just accept this bit of luck and take the win.

I did another tour around the house and, on my second pass through the back yard, I heard something that sounded like crying.

It was soft, but my ears were keen and I focused for a moment to pin-point it. It sounded like it was coming from the line of bikes covered by heavy tarps. We didn't have fancy bike covers, only camping tarps, which we used to keep the elements off our prized machines. The four bikes in the yard were set up in pairs and I zeroed in on one of the pairs. I lifted the tarp, pulling up the piton which had been sunk into the ground at one corner.

And there, wedged between the two bikes — Tank's and Brick's — was Petra. She was naked and sitting with her knees pulled up in front of her. Her one wrist was hand-cuffed to Tank's bike.

I swallowed the bile that rose in the back of my throat. My father was an animal. Completely inhuman. How could he leave a pregnant woman out here, naked and cold?

I ground my teeth so hard I couldn't speak. I went to her and grabbed the handcuffs, prying the metal links apart until they snapped, freeing her from the bike.

"I've got you now," I whispered. "I'll make sure *he* never gets his hands on you ever again." I picked her up and didn't bother covering the bikes when I left.

I looked around as I crossed the back yard, my mind

edgy. Where was my father? Tank didn't usually let Petra get too far from him. I sniffed the air. His scent was all over the back yard, hard to pin down. Mostly his scent covered Petra and I had trouble tracing it anywhere else.

I'd find him later. Right now, I needed to get Petra to safety before he returned from wherever he'd gone. It couldn't have been far... his bike was still here. Maybe he'd gone for a wander in the forest?

I brought Petra around to the side door, not the back. I easily cradled her in one arm while I opened the door, then hurried her downstairs into the basement.

"Kira!" I hissed as I reached the rec room. "Keep Petra safe!" I put the shaken woman down on the long couch in the rec room. Kira instantly covered her with a blanket.

"Think you can stop Tank if he comes for her?" I asked.

"If she can't, I will," Dana Juarez said, her tone icy.

"We all will," Cassie said, voice trembling even as she showed a surprising spirit and strength with her words. "He's not getting his hands on her again!"

I almost wanted Tank to come for Petra. I was curious what these three she-wolves could do to him, even though it wouldn't be a pretty fight.

In truth, I was hoping I got my hands on him first. It was time he learned what it felt like to be beaten into submission. I wouldn't kill him, even if that's what he deserved, but breaking a few bones didn't seem out of the question.

I heard another bike rumble to life in the distance.

All of us in the rec room tilted our heads, listening. With exceptional hearing and years around all of these bikes, we could usually identify each bike by its sound. This was Sonny's Fat Boy. I relaxed a little. Not my father. Though, perhaps Sonny knew where I could find him.

Sonny was the quiet one of Harley's old betas, the youngest and lowest in rank. He hadn't been causing a lot of trouble for Jane, and I was starting to hope that maybe he was a decent guy. He'd done his fair share of nasty things with the gang, but perhaps that was just to prove he was as tough as the others.

I started up the stairs, taking them two at a time. The sound of Sonny's bike got closer. He was leaving, coming from the back, around the side of the house, to the driveway.

I reached the side door and opened it just as Sonny stopped where the driveway ended toward the back of the house.

He dug around in a heavy looking satchel slung over his shoulder and pulled out something, which looked heavy, a large rock perhaps? He only then looked up and saw me. He cocked a smile then winked. Throwing that stone toward the house, he gunned his bike and sped toward me.

Too much happened at once, I watched the rock shatter the window to Jane's bedroom and wanted to run and check on that, but Sonny was aiming to run me down. I dove out of the way and rolled along the asphalt driveway, coming up on one knee as Sonny raced by, laughing maniacally. So much for Sonny potentially being a decent guy.

He pulled another large stone out of the satchel. I was torn. I wanted to go check on Jane, but... the broken window wasn't close to her bed and the worst that could have happened was that she'd have a draft. That could easily be fixed. Also, Tyson was with her and Bronn close by.

With a growl, I wrenched my attention away from the window and went after Sonny. By the time I'd reached the front of the house, Sonny had thrown a rock through the front kitchen window and was tossing another through the large bay window in the living area.

He spun his bike around, tearing up more of what little grass remained on Jane's front lawn.

He pulled out another stone and tossed it through another section of that large bay window, even as he gunned his bike again, heading for me.

"Ride or die!" he shouted as he drew close.

This time I was prepared, I didn't dive out of the way. Instead, I stepped to the side at the last second, extending my arm to hit Sonny mid chest. That knocked him off his bike, but also tore a few muscles in my shoulder. I winced at the pain, but it would heal quick enough.

Sonny landed on his back with a surprised "Oof!" and there was a loud crash behind me.

"Fuck," I hissed, spinning around.

And there was Sonny's bike T-boned into Jane's car.

"What the fuck!" I recognized Bronn's voice as I turned back. Bronn had the front door of the house open. "What's going on out here?" he called.

Sonny just laughed as he got up. "I didn't think it would actually work, but Brick was right!" He seemed far too happy that his bike was totaled. A creeping dread clawed at my gut. This had all been planned, but... to what end?

Then it hit me, with Bronn and I here, who was watching Jane's door?

I took a hesitant step toward the house. My next step was at a dead run. "Bronn, get back inside!" I yelled.

I saw the realization dawn on him. This had been a distraction, drawing him away from his post.

From inside the house came a roar I knew all too well. My father as a bear.

Bronn spun in the doorway. "Fuck!"

I reached the front door in time to see Tank, as a massive bear, bursting through the door into Jane's bedroom.

My heart leaped into my throat. No... he couldn't... he wouldn't dare try to harm Jane before the week was up, would he? With my father, you never knew. He was a savage and unstable man.

Bronn and I raced in, but we were too far away to stop him.

It was up to Tyson now.

TYSON

I ROSE TO MY FEET, FURIOUS AT THE ROCK THAT HAD COME crashing through Jane's window. Hearing Sonny's Fat Boy speed away, I suspected Brick was up to something, but I couldn't leave Jane, not now. The moon was up. She'd shift at any moment.

I headed to the hall so I could ask Bronn to check in with Colt and see if he'd seen anything on his patrols. But I didn't make it to the door.

Jane gave a muffled cry. I spun back. She was starting to shift... or trying to. It didn't look right at all.

"Fuck," I hissed.

I should have had Dana and Nico up here with me. They knew what a first shift was like for a late-in-life convert and could tell me if this was normal. My experiences with a first shift were with natural born wolves, as teens. It was awkward and painful, but their body knew what it needed to do. The virus had been in their blood for years and was only just finally making itself complete, taking its other form.

But for someone who'd just been turned and only had the virus in their system for a short time... perhaps their body didn't know what to do quite yet? I didn't know.

Jane jerked and flailed so wildly the sheets were thrown off her. A ripple ran over her body, from toes to head, seemingly breaking every bone. Skin jutted and jumped in ways it definitely shouldn't. Her body seemed to be trying to split in two, right down the middle.

The sound of bones snapping and reforming so fast like popcorn was horrific. The sight almost made me sick.

This didn't look right at all.

Her constant scream became a horrid wet gurgling as her face twisted and tried to reform. Her eyes flared with agony, shifting from her dark-caramel brown to wolfen yellow and back.

I wanted — No, I *needed* — to help her, but I didn't know how!

I ran to her, desperate to do something, even if it was just pulling her away from cracking her skull on the headboard. I managed to grab her head, pulling her to the side before she hurt herself. Under my hands, her skull shuddered and shifted, trying to stretch, but then snapped back into place.

Fur rippled out of her skin in spots only to vanish again and appear elsewhere, like some wild patchwork. One of her legs was half-shifted, somewhere between wolf and human, as was one of her arms.

"Fuck me," I whispered.

It hadn't occurred to me that I might lose Jane here and now from some inability to make the transformation.

I'd assumed she'd shift just fine and it would be Brick's challenge next week we'd have to worry about. But it looked like she was breaking in all the wrong ways.

Her face elongated again, her snout forming, and this time stayed, as fur rippled over it in patches. A wolfen whine escaped her. She was close. There was nothing I could do, other than be there for her, so I knelt next to the bed and hoped.

Then the door to Jane's room was torn off its hinges as Tank-as-a-bear lumbered in and roared. I couldn't help it, fear surged through me. Bears were one of the few animals wolves feared... especially one on one.

Time seemed to stretch, my reactions far too slow.

I reached for Jane to hold her, protect her, but she jerked out of my reach. With a scream, which turned to a howling-whine, her body spasmed one last time and she shifted.

Her wolf was beautiful: a golden-brown coat over the sides and rump, with a white belly and darker stripes of brown over her shoulders and on her face. She had a white patch around her mouth and black lines framing her eyes. Eyes filled with raw terror as Tank's bear roared again.

Tank had scared her into shifting. Had he meant to do that?

Yet my joy was short-lived. Jane's wolf bolted. She leaped from the bed to the dresser, then out the broken window, crashing through the remaining glass.

Gone.

And suddenly it all fell into place.

Breaking her window hadn't just been an act of petty

vandalism. It had been so Jane's wolf would smell the evening air and see that as an escape from the bear charging her. And that's exactly what she'd done.

I rose to go after her, but Tank lumbered closer. I tore at my clothes, needing to shift now! But I had no time. Cloth ripped as I shifted to my hybrid form. It would be the only way I *might* have a chance against Tank-as-a-bear. There wasn't enough room in here for him to take his mid-form. Hell, he'd broken the doorframe just squeezing through the door to get in as a bear.

Tank swiped at me, and I leaped back, narrowly avoiding his massive claws.

Then Tank roared again, but this time it was in pain. Through the broken doorway, I caught glimpses of a lion jumping onto Tank's back.

Thank you, Bronn.

I shifted into my wolf — what remained of my clothes fell away from this smaller form — and followed Jane out the window. The bits of jagged glass that remained cut at my flanks, but I didn't care.

I paused on the driveway outside. The sun had set, but there was still light enough to see. No sign of Jane. What I did see was Sonny, coming from the front of the house, stalking up the driveway toward me... gun in his hand.

"Can't challenge the alpha, but we *can* kill you," he said, firing.

The first bullet caught my hip, but only a grazing, glancing blow. I bolted toward the back yard, bullets flying around me. One tore off the top of one ear, which was far from fatal but stung like hell. Another hit a hind leg. It wasn't a bad blow, but it would slow me down.

Whatever the old betas had planned, it seemed to be working. More crashing and roaring came from inside the house. Tank still fought. I wished Bronn luck and hoped Colt was there to help him. Meanwhile, I was on the defensive and Jane was who-knew-where! I needed to find her, but first I needed to deal with Sonny.

Once I was around the back of the house, I shifted back to human. Pain surged at the side of my face, my hip, and leg. I grunted, steeling myself as I looked for a weapon. I hobbled over to one of the tarps. The corner was already pulled up and I grabbed the loose piton. That would have to do.

Turning back, I saw Sonny coming around the back of the house. He fired again. A bullet grazed my arm as I charged at him.

I ducked under two more shots, then the slide of his gun caught and the trigger clicked. He was out of ammo.

With a roar, I reached him and knocked the gun away with one hand while stabbing the piton into his gut with the other. He grunted and went down as I fell on top of him. I rolled away quickly, but he didn't come after me. Sonny yowled and laughed in turns.

"It's... too late..." he hissed through the pain. "You ain't never... gonna see... that bitch again!"

"Like hell," I growled. I'd find her if it was the last thing I did.

I shifted again and ran for the front of the house, hoping to pick up Jane's scent. She smelled a bit different as a wolf. There was the same aroma of dewy grasses, but the smell of sun-on-skin had become that of warmed fur. I picked it up quickly and followed it, as fast as the searing pain in my hip and leg would allow.

I'd find her. I'd find my fated and help her through this transition. I swore it on my life... because if I lost her... there wouldn't be a reason for me to keep living.

BRONN

IN MY HYBRID FORM, IT WAS HARD TO MANEUVER IN THE back hallway of Jane's house. But thankfully it was even harder for Tank-as-a-bear, and impossible for him to take his mid-form here. Luckily, Colt and I had him trapped between us. Unluckily, Tank was facing in my direction, trying to get past me to the back door. The fact that that door was still there meant Tank had snuck in as a human. He must have shifted just as he knocked down Jane's bedroom door.

I roared, swatting one of his massive claws away with my own, scoring the back of his paw. He surged forward to bite me and I danced back, swatting his face, my claws scoring lines down his snout.

"What the fuck is going on out—" Rita opened the door to Izzy's room. She was behind Tank, next to Colt. "Fuck me!"

With a growl, she shifted into her mid-form and roared at Tank.

Tank charged me.

I leaped up, hoping Jane would forgive me for the deep claw marks I left in her ceiling as I held myself up there so the bear could rush by beneath me. I released myself quickly, dropping behind Tank as he smashed through the back door and out into the yard. I followed with preternatural speed with Colt and Rita close behind me.

Tank spun to face us, shifting into his hybrid form, horrifying as all hell. Colt did the same beside me, making me feel a lot better. Now it was a wolf, a lion, and a bear against just one bear and Tank knew it.

A pained shout caused me to turn. Sonny was nearby, stripping so he could shift, but he had a bloody gash in his stomach slowing him. I decided to take him out so he wouldn't be able to help Tank.

One leap and I reached him. He was mid-shift, which should have only lasted an instant, but he was weak and wavering. One swipe of my claws opened his belly, enough to keep him out of the fight, but with our enhanced healing it *probably* wouldn't kill him. Howling with pain, Sonny fell back reverting to human form.

One down.

I turned back to see Colt and Tank locked together in a scary-as-fuck bear fight. Rita kept to the fringes, finding small openings to dart in and nip at Tank.

We all wanted Tank gone. He was a loathsome plague on shifter-kind and humanity, but we couldn't kill him. Jane had made it clear. We didn't kill our own. I was fairly certain Jane would make an exception for Tank, but then... she was just kind-hearted enough that I wasn't sure. That meant we had to take down Tank without killing him: just maim him, break a few bones, that sort of thing.

I wanted to roar, but I knew my best advantage was stealth. I padded around, getting behind Tank as Colt lined him up for me.

I was terrified — on a visceral, primal level — for so many reasons. First, that bear was twice the size I was. Second, Tank and Brick had beaten me so much, it was practically ingrained in me to defer to them.

But Tank had crossed a line. He'd gone after our alpha, an alpha I hoped with all my heart could change all of our lives for the better.

Pushing past my fear, I leaped and came down on Tank's back. I caught his thick neck in my jaws and I bit hard. At the same time, I sunk my heavy claws into his shoulders and raked across that broad back. Colt had Tank's arms occupied, keeping them in place as the two of them wrestled with roughly equal strength.

I kept my hold on Tank's neck while releasing my claws, then sinking them in again, this time front and back claws both raked down that heavy body. Tank roared in pain.

Good.

I could have killed him in that moment. A bit more strength behind my bite and I'd break his neck, but I didn't, for Jane. Instead, I tossed myself backward with a flip, landing lightly.

Tank staggered and stumbled, losing the war of strength against his son.

I glanced at Rita and it was like our thoughts merged.

We both looked at Tank's thick legs then back to each other, nodding.

We rushed in low, each biting Tank close to the ankle, our teeth tearing and ripping as Colt pushed him back. I felt the bone break under my crushing teeth, then darted away.

Tank fell, shifting and screaming bloody murder as he became a man once again.

The fight was over, Tank had lost and would be laid up for a while, but Colt wasn't finished with his father. Still in his mid-form, Colt leaned down and gave a swipe at Tanks belly. Those thick claws grazed Tank's stomach, but that hadn't been what Colt was aiming for. Instead, half of Tank's cock came flying off and the big man's scream shot up two octaves.

I smiled as a righteous justice settled within me. Tank was a brute and a letch. This seemed a fitting punishment for him.

Rita hobbled over to us, wounded, but mostly well.

Colt and I reverted to our human forms.

"Jane?" he asked quickly.

"I don't know," I said. "I think Tyson went after her."

"Go! Find her!" Rita shouted at us. But we weren't going to be going anywhere as naked men and it was too light out to be trotting down the street as a lion and a bear. We quickly scrambled back inside to find some clothes.

"Hang on, Jane!" I whispered to myself. "We're coming!"

JANE

NOTHING MADE SENSE. MY MIND SPUN. SOMEWHERE DEEP in the recesses of my soul screamed a part of me that used to be... something else, and that sliver of myself knew this was wrong.

Except all *I* knew for certain was that there had been a horrible beast. I'd gotten away from it, but I'd crashed through something that had cut deep gashes along my flanks. Yet that pain was secondary to my raging hunger. I was bombarded with powerful scents all around me, but one in particular called to me: a fresh kill, blood, somewhere in that forest.

So, I ran...

...away from that terrifying beast...

...urged by my starvation...

...toward the smell of blood.

I knew if I just followed my nose, I'd find it, and I'd sink my fangs into warm flesh and tear and bite and devour. That was what I was meant to do: hunt, kill, consume.

I just wished the pain slicing through me would go away. I could smell my own blood. I didn't know how I knew it was my blood, but given the pain it made sense.

My right arm — no, it was a leg — had been cut when I'd fled from that strange cave where the beast had come for me. There was also pain along my sides, as well as one other leg. Still, I ran as fast as I could through the darkening woods toward that wonderful scent of meat.

Then it came into view. A small doe. Something else had killed it but had left it mostly intact. The scent of that warm blood filled my nostrils and sent a rumble like thunder through my gut. I reached the animal and instinctively went for the neck. That was already torn open, where the most blood was spilled. I didn't care, I tore at it again, feeling the metallic warmth splash on my tongue.

I'd never tasted anything so delicious in my life. Admittedly, it had been a very short life, starting in that strange cave. I remembered precious little before that... only hazy memories, which didn't seem like my own.

I moved from the neck to the soft belly, tearing that open and devouring everything that spilled out. It was a glorious feast. I couldn't eat fast enough, couldn't get enough into my famished body.

My ears swiveled, picking up the sounds of movement and a growl.

Danger! I knew this instinctively. My head came up, eyes scanning the dark beneath the trees. There! A blond wolf, fangs bared, snarling, slowly pacing through the forest, making a wide circle around me.

I snarled back.

This was *my* kill... well I hadn't made the kill, but it was mine now and I'd defend it. I hadn't sated my cavernous hunger yet. If this other wolf got in the way, I'd devour them too.

Though, as much as I knew how to run and eat, I didn't really know how to fight. My short life had consisted of running in fear, then running toward food.

My teeth could score and rend. I'd use them... somehow. I should go for the neck. That seemed to make sense. But something told me this other wolf had lived a life much longer than mine and knew what it was doing... what... *she* was doing. I could smell her now that she was upwind of me. I wasn't sure what part of her scent identified her as female, I just *knew*.

Her bark was a warning, a threat. I understood it implicitly even though I'd never heard a bark before. It meant *you're dead* or *I'll kill you*, something along those lines, the meaning clear enough to my mind.

I barked back, *Mine! Go away!*

The she-wolf gave a whuffing sound of amusement. She wasn't afraid of me. Yet she waited, pacing back and forth, wary. I kept my eyes on her. She wasn't smart. As long as she was upwind of me, not only would I see her coming, but I'd smell her too.

It was my ears that saved me. I heard the crunch of rushing paws behind me, close. Only then did I realize that the bitch had been a distraction, keeping my focus upwind so I wouldn't smell her partner.

I dove to the side with a whine and yelp as a larger wolf dove at me, jaws open and snarling. This one was a big, grey male, with loathing in his yellow eyes. He'd barely landed when he nimbly launched himself at me again.

I shifted my weight to the side, trying to nip at him as he passed by, but I missed. I'd never done this before. The large grey clearly had.

His nip caught my shoulder. I yowled in pain as he spun again, keeping close, jaws snapping, going for my throat. He kept his head low, so I couldn't do the same, forcing me to scramble back.

Then something bowled me over from the side: the she-wolf. She landed on top of me, pinning me down. Her teeth tore at my flank. The big grey came for my throat. I ducked my head and he caught my snout instead. His teeth tore into my tender flesh and I whined, losing strength.

I thrashed, desperate to get away. I snapped back at the grey once he'd released me, but nothing seemed to work. I was too weak, injured, and hungry. I was also far less experienced than these two.

The she-wolf sank her teeth into my right-hind leg, deep. She released me only to bite that same paw, hard, crippling it. Then she jumped back, off me.

The two moved back for a moment, both barking and making that whuffing sound of amusement. Their intentions were clear: *run little wolf, we want to hunt you. Give us the thrill of a chase and maybe we'll end you quickly.*

They were playing with me.

I rose slowly. I could barely stand. Agony arched through every part of me and my right-hind-leg couldn't support me. I wouldn't get far on only three legs.

Then something solidified inside me. Some part of

me knew that I had pups... somewhere... to live for. I had a life, another life, a strange life. And I needed to get back to that life. I needed to live. And running would only tire me more. My only option was to stand and fight, here and now. I didn't know how I could win, but I had to try. I'd die here, if that was my fate.

My fate...

Fate...?

Fated...

The image of a wolf came to mind, dark fur with splashes of white. I knew that wolf like they were a part of me even though I was certain I'd never actually seen them before. This was my mate, and he would come for me, find me. He had to. If he didn't... my short life would end far too soon.

I barked my challenge: *Come and get me.*

The big grey barked once, *Fool!*

Fool I may be, but I wouldn't run. This ended now, one way or another.

The big grey charged in, the she-wolf circling, ready to strike.

I barked and crouched low, ready...

TYSON

I SMELLED A FRESH KILL AHEAD OF ME ALONG WITH THREE wolves. Two of them, I'd know anywhere, I'd known their scents all my life: Brick and Ginny. The third was the one I'd been following, the scent of wet grass and warm fur: Jane.

Everything clicked into place. Brick and Ginny leaving had only been a ruse to lull us into a false sense of security, and they hadn't gone far. They'd hunted the doe to lure Jane into their clutches, knowing she would be drawn by hunger. Sonny had shattered the window to let in the evening air, and Tank had barged in to scare her out. Jane would scent the kill and fall right into their trap and Brick and Ginny would maul her then leave her for dead and no one would be able to prove it was them. Every move had been carefully orchestrated to corner her in their cunning, vicious plot.

My heart pounded, adrenaline surging through my veins and numbing the pain of my own wounds. The scent of blood, mingled with Jane's alluring fragrance, filled my senses and ignited an urgency to protect her at all costs.

Following the trail of her blood, I raced through the forest in my wolf form. I knew she was wounded, vulnerable and inexperienced as a wolf, which made her a perfect target for Brick and Ginny.

Trees melted into a frantic blur as the scent of the kill and the sounds of the fight drew nearer. Barks cut through the forest's stillness, the first a challenge to run. Brick and Ginny wanted to hunt Jane for sport like the merciless predators they were.

Then came Jane's defiant reply, *Come and get me.* Determination laced her tone, daring them to come after her, and my heart twisted with pride and fear. What was she thinking? If she ran, she'd prolong her life, at least for a moment, giving me time to get to her. But if she couldn't run...

Fuck!

I pushed my body even harder, muscles straining as I raced through the woods, leaping over obstacles and ignoring the stinging branches that whipped against my fur.

One last bark, from Brick, *Fool!*

My breath caught, dread clawing at my guts.

No!

Time seemed to slow, dragging like an eternity, until I finally reached the small clearing. My gaze locked on Jane's wolf, her beautiful form hunkered low, growling, and covered in blood. Shards of glass were still stuck in her sides, her right rear leg had been brutally mauled, and there was far too much blood staining her snout.

And yet, she refused to back down, confronting these two vicious predators with unwavering bravery. *This* was the woman who'd faced Harley and killed him.

I may have been fated for her — my love inevitable — but my heart still surged with devotion and admiration for her stalwart bravery in the face of overwhelming odds.

Brick charged her.

I was faster and he was too focused on her to notice me. I hit him side-long and sunk my teeth into his flank, tearing away flesh as I tackled him to the ground.

But he wasn't the only threat. Ginny charged at Jane. Jane shifted to face the new threat, but Ginny caught Jane's neck. Luckily, it was the back, not the throat. Ginny thrashed and Jane — weakened as she was — was tossed to the ground. Ginny released Jane, going for her throat, but I was already leaping. I caught Ginny's snout and bit deep, drawing a yelp and whine. I released her and she quickly backed off.

Snarling, I stood over Jane, waiting for the two of them to come at me.

Brick rose, clearly hesitating now that he was wounded. That chunk I'd taken out of his side wasn't going to kill him, but it would hurt like hell and hinder him in this fight. Ginny, however, wasn't dissuaded by her pain. She came at me, even as Brick barked to call her off.

We both went for the other's neck and the result was our jaws clacking together in a mash of teeth.

Ginny backed away.

Brick repeated his bark for her to stop.

She growled at me again before she swung her head

to look at Brick. Then the two of them slowly backed away. Perhaps they thought they'd done enough damage to Jane already.

In truth, they might have.

There came a broken and half-hearted whine below me, but I stayed where I was, keeping Brick and Ginny in sight until they'd faded into the forest. My keen ears caught them circling us, staying close, but another whine drew my attention down to see Jane's yellow eyes pleading with me. That last attack from Ginny had been brutal, deep rents scoring Jane's neck and welling with blood.

Jane gave a huffing whine then barked softly, *Mate?*

Somehow, even though she'd only been a wolf for a short time — and never seen me as a wolf — she knew me.

I barked my reply, *Yes, mate.* I licked her snout.

She licked me back, a thank you, then whined again. *So much pain.*

I gave a comforting whuff. *I know. I'm here now. I'll help you.*

She laid her head on the ground, her eyes fluttering shut. With me here, she felt safe enough to rest, but I feared she might never wake. I needed to get her help. Now.

Except Brick and Ginny were still out there, and I couldn't leave her alone to fetch help. I couldn't do anything for her. My wolf form could protect her, but not help her. Perhaps, if I shifted back to human, I could carry her to safety.

Except I'd be naked and vulnerable.

My only option was my hybrid form.

I shifted, praying it would be enough to keep Brick and Ginny away. Though if they decided to take their hybrid forms...

Then I'd do what I had to.

The transformation was taxing, draining my already weakened body, but I had no other choice. My instincts screamed at me to protect Jane at any cost.

Thankfully, Brick and Ginny didn't attack. I could only guess they were waiting for me to falter since it wasn't easy to sustain a mid-form. It required a lot of high emotions. Luckily, I had those in spades: fear for my fated, hatred for Brick and the others. Most of all, I had my boundless affection for this fierce and caring woman who had turned my life upside down in the best possible way.

Carefully, I lifted Jane's limp wolf, being mindful of my long sharp claws. A soft, breathy whine escaped her, and relief washed over me. She was still breathing, still alive. That was all that mattered.

Holding her close to my chest, I started the long walk through the woods.

I didn't know what I'd do once I was out of the forest and back on the street. Walking around like this was asking for trouble. But I couldn't think about that. For now, I held my love close and forged ahead...

...as wolves howled around me.

Don't miss the next book in the series!

Want You Pack
Her Bad Boy Wolves: Book Two

Yesterday I was a suburban working mother, today I'm an alpha wolf with a pack to tame.

I may be plain-old Jane Myers, but I'm no longer your average forty-something mother of two. Now, I'm a wolf shifter, though my first shift definitely didn't go as planned. A few in my new pack don't like me being the alpha and tried to skirt around my one-week proving period by attacking me as a wolf during my first run.

Thankfully, my huge and hunky betas saved me.

But I'm seriously hurt and the only way to heal me quickly is to make me go into heat. So now my betas are serving me in an entirely different capacity. The young bear shifter Colt is a mountain of muscle I can't wait to climb. Bronn, my beautiful, black-skinned lion shifter, is tender and kind, even when he's thrilling me beyond measure. And last, but definitely not least is Tyson, the tall, dark, and dangerous wolf who is fated for me. When we come together it's primal and searingly hot. I hadn't known about knots before, but I do now!

And I still need to deal with those bad seeds who are trying to claim the pack, but that means I have less than a week to learn how to fight as a wolf, or I'm dead meat.

OTHER BOOKS BY TESSA COLE

Wolf Decided, book 5

Wolf Devoted, book 6

THE GRECIAN GODDESS TRILOGY

Co-written with Clara Wils

Kiss of the Goddess, book 1

Power of the Goddess, book 2

Bonds of the Goddess, book 3

THE SECRETS GODS KEEP

Co-written with Clara Wils

Craving Demons, book 1

Chaos Demons, book 2

Claiming Demons, book 3

HER BAD BOY WOLVES

Co-written with Clara Wils

Pack to the Wall, book 1

Want you Pack, book 2

Pack in Business, book 3

OTHER BOOKS BY CLARA WILS

THE GRECIAN GODDESS TRILOGY

Co-written with Tessa Cole

Kiss of the Goddess, book 1

Power of the Goddess, book 2

Bonds of the Goddess, book 3

THE MISTS OF ELISTA TRILOGY

Bonds and Blood, book 1

Shape and Shadows, book 2

Form and Fury, book 3

SISTER SPIRITS

Double Discover, book 1

Double Danger, book 2

Double Disaster, book 3

Double Doom, book 4

Double Destiny, book 5

THE SECRETS GODS KEEP

Co-written with Tessa Cole

Craving Demons, book 1

Chaos Demons, book 2

Claiming Demons, book 3

HER BAD BOY WOLVES

Co-written with Tessa Cole

Pack to the Wall, book 1

Want you Pack, book 2

Pack in Business, book 3